RESCUING ANNIE

Delta Force Heroes Series

SUSAN STOKER

3 0646 00244 5066

CHAPTER ONE

Captain Ann Fletcher looked around, struggling to understand how everything had gone to shit so quickly. She and her Green Beret Special Forces squad had gone out to do some reconnaissance...and somehow found themselves in the middle of a firefight.

They'd arrived in eastern Afghanistan a week ago and had spent the time since getting caught up with the layout of the area and their target's movements and followers. A raid was in the planning stage for ten days from now. Ann and her squad were going to lead about a hundred Afghani commandos in an attempt to kill or capture Sahib Lal Wakil. He was the newest leader of the local Taliban group, and one of the most brutal. Reports alleged that he hadn't hesitated to kill his own son, who'd contradicted him in front of his followers.

Ann and her squad had arrived in the country and immediately gotten to work meeting with Afghani officials, trying to come up with the best way to get to Wakil. He was holed up in a small town in the middle of a large mountain range. Getting to him wouldn't be easy as the location he'd chosen for his home base was almost impossible to approach without notice. The quickest way to get to the location was by helicopter, but as soon as the chopper got anywhere near the location, Wakil and his followers would know, which made it extremely risky. Despite the risk, the information that would be gathered on the location of Wakil's men and how many followers the terrorist actually had would be invaluable to defeating him once and for all.

Today was supposed to be a recon of the valley they'd have to cross just to *get* to the village where Wakil was located. But the simple reconnaissance had turned into a full-blown firefight.

The team had been dropped off without incident, but shortly after they began to make their way across, they'd been attacked by heavy artillery fire while in the narrow valley and had retreated up the side of the mountain, opposite of where Wakil's forces had taken up positions. While they'd been engaging the insurgents, Wakil had sent some of his men closer to the Green Beret's position, effectively surrounding them and cutting them off from any retreat. It was taking everything Ann and her team had to keep from being picked off one by one.

As it was, two of Ann's six teammates had been injured and there seemed to be no lessening of the attack. They were making their shots count, and not firing indiscriminately, but for every insurgent they took out, it seemed another immediately took his place.

"Bell! Did you get a hold of air support?" Ann yelled.

"Ten-four!" Sergeant Charlie Bell shouted back,

straining to be heard above the sounds of gunfire the others were laying down. "Two minutes and counting!"

Ann nodded as she concentrated on tightening the tourniquet around Green's leg. She had the most medical experience out of everyone on the team, and had taken it upon herself to do what she could for her teammate. Keeping one eye open for the enemy, she divided her attention between working on Green and making sure no one tried to climb up to the ridge where they'd taken refuge. Green had been hit in the knee by a sniper bullet. Her tourniquet was doing what it was supposed to, namely keeping him from bleeding to death, but he definitely would need more intensive medical attention.

Unfortunately, the longer they stayed on this ridge, the higher the chance none of them would make it out alive. Shef's left arm had been taken out of commission by one of the snipers as well, but luckily he was right-handed and he hadn't stopped firing back.

Bits and pieces of rock flew all around them as bullets hit the mountainside. The air was heavy with dust as the shots hit rocks and dirt, making it harder and harder to see the enemy, but that also made it more difficult for others to see *them*, which could work in their favor. Still, Ann needed their air support to get there *now*. They might not have two minutes. The team was literally sitting ducks. They were spread out along the ridge, doing their best to use the large boulders as cover as they returned fire, trying to take out the snipers.

Seven Special Forces soldiers against who knew how many terrorists weren't good odds. All it would take was one rocket-propelled grenade and they'd all be blown to bits.

Amazingly, Ann didn't panic. Instead, her concentration sharpened. The volley of gunfire faded into the background as she made sure the tourniquet on Green's leg was holding. When she was done, the sergeant didn't hesitate to get right back into the fray. Ann could smell Green's blood that had seeped into her uniform and smeared on her hands. She smelled her own sweat and the stench of the dirt and sand. It seemed as if the worse the odds got, the more steady she became.

"Twenty seconds!" Bell shouted, warning everyone that the shit was about to hit the fan.

Ann knew as well as anyone that the chances of them getting out of this clusterfuck alive was slim to none. Even with air support coming in to drop artillery on the coordinates Bell gave the pilots, being extracted wasn't guaranteed.

Even so, the sound of the Blackhawk helicopters coming in hot and hard over the ridge toward them was as sweet as anything Ann had ever heard. The firepower the helicopters laid down was impressive, and scary. The airstrikes were coming way too close to their location for comfort, but it was necessary to keep the insurgents from overrunning their position.

———

Four hours later, all seven of the Green Berets were wounded in one way or another. The helicopters had done their job, keeping the insurgents from overrunning their position. The fire they were taking had lessened, but not enough for Ann's team to safely extricate themselves on foot. The enemy snipers were still doing their best to pick them off and that, along with the injuries the team had suffered, made a chopper the only way for them to get out of the area.

Green wasn't doing well and should've been extracted hours ago. Ann had wanted to stay on the move, making it harder for the snipers to hit their mark, but with the injuries sustained by her team, it was a better idea to stay put. She'd done her best to keep Green comfortable, even as he and Shef continued to fight.

Joe had slipped on the rocks, resulting in bruised or broken ribs. She knew the guys would give him shit for that for years to come. Gabe had been grazed in the head by a sniper. If he hadn't turned to look at Green at the last second, the bullet would've gone right through his forehead. Bell's right hand had taken a direct hit. He'd been signing to Gabe and one of the enemy snipers had gotten in a lucky shot. Mack had also been hit, but the bullet had gone through the fleshy part of his upper arm.

Ann herself hadn't gotten away unscathed. She and Bell had been scrambling to switch positions as Wakil's men crept closer during a lull in the air strikes and she'd tripped. It was stupid; she was running and had simply lost her footing, slamming her forehead into the ground. She was never going to live that down, but she wouldn't mind the ribbing from her teammates if she made it out alive. Even with her Kevlar helmet on, she'd torn off a good chunk of skin over her eyebrow. She'd been dealing with blood dripping into her eye ever since. But that hadn't stopped her from taking out her fair share of insurgents.

Finally, it was time to get the hell out. The extraction from their current position wasn't going to be easy. The choppers would take a lot of enemy fire and Ann and her team would be exposed. But dusk was setting in, and they needed to get out of there before it was completely dark. Wakil's men knew this land much better than they did, and while the darkness could cover the team's movements, possibly allowing them to sneak out, it would do the same for the enemy, allowing them to ambush the Green Berets.

As the highest-ranking soldier of the group, Ann was used to making decisions for the team. She didn't always like doing so, but she never shirked her duty.

"When the first chopper comes in, I'll take Green while, Mack, you and Gabe lay down cover fire for us. Joe, I need you to help Shef," Ann told her team. "It looks like there will be two separate extractions. With the number of door gunners necessary, we won't all fit in one chopper. Once the first helo is gone, we'll reassess and Bell will coordinate with the second team of Night Stalkers. There will only be a few minutes between choppers, so we won't be waiting for long. We're all gonna get out of here. Together. Hear me?"

"Fuck yeah, we are."

"Yes, Ma'am."

"I missed lunch."

Ann couldn't stop the chuckle that rose up at Mack's words. He was always hungry. It wasn't too surprising as he was a big son-of-a-bitch. She was just glad she wouldn't have to carry his ass out of here. She was strong, but at over two hundred and fifty pounds to her one fifty, Green would be a challenge to extract.

Thirty minutes later, it was time. As far as she was concerned, the Night Stalker helicopter pilots were the true heroes in any kind of firefight. They were always a target for RPG attacks and she'd seen some amazing flying abilities from the men and women who were behind the controls of the huge machines. Today was no exception.

The valley where they'd been doing reconnaissance was narrow, and while they'd climbed up the side of the steep terrain behind them, getting out of the valley and somewhat evening the odds against the insurgents, the pilots would have their work cut out for them, making sure they didn't get too close to the mountainside.

The pilot was hovering near an outcropping of rocks, keeping the chopper steady as the door gunners laid down enough firepower to make even the most tenacious of snipers take cover. It was a precarious position; a gust of wind could shift the chopper, making the rotor blades hit the mountain, which was only feet away.

But Ann had no time to admire the bravery and flying ability of the pilot and gunners. She needed to get Green inside so he could receive advanced medical care. Too much time had passed since he'd been shot. Frustration hit her. She was a damn good medic, and she hated that she couldn't do more for him.

Signing to her team that it was go time, Ann hefted Sergeant Green over her shoulder and took the lead as she ran as fast as she could toward the idling chopper. Joe and Shef ran behind her. Mack, Gabe, and Bell covered them, as did the soldiers inside the chopper, the bullets flying fast and furious.

Before she knew it, Ann was at the extraction point. She practically threw Green inside the helicopter, relieved when the two door gunners got him safely situated, then turned to help Joe and Shef.

The second they were in, the chopper tilted away from the mountain and flew hard and fast.

Ann felt more than heard a bullet whiz by her head. She dropped to her belly and crawled backward toward the dubious safety of a boulder.

The echo of gunfire was loud, easily heard over the sound of the chopper rising into the sky. Looking toward Bell, Mack, and Gabe, she gave them the signal that she was all right, that she hadn't been hit. When she received the corresponding signal back saying the same, she breathed out a sigh of relief. Three down, three to go.

Ann took the safety of her team seriously. In the five and a half years that she'd been in the Army, she'd lost her share of men under her command. And each one left a hole in her heart. She'd do what it took to get these men extracted.

No one would say Captain Fletcher wasn't qualified to be a Green Beret. She'd worked her ass off to get here, her journey paved by women like Aspen Mesmer, now Aspen Temple. Aspen had been one of the first female combat medics attached to a Ranger unit and had gone through absolute hell to prove that she could do the job just as well as a man.

Taking a deep breath, Ann concentrated on her current situation. They were now three men down as far as firepower went. They were at their most vulnerable as they waited for the second extraction chopper. She knew as well as her men that the second extraction would be twice as dangerous as the first. Wakil's men knew what to expect now. And they'd be even more desperate to make sure they didn't escape.

Staying on her belly, and grateful for the dust the chopper's rotors had kicked up in the air, giving her additional cover, Ann crawled her way back to where Bell was both returning fire and manning their communication radio. "How long?" she asked.

"Four," Bell said stiffly.

Shit. Four minutes was an eternity. But Ann simply nodded. She was too well trained to show any dismay to those under her command.

The next four minutes were the longest of her life. The shots were getting closer as Wakil's followers crept nearer to their location, as if they knew this was their last chance to kill or capture their enemies.

The plan was for the Blackhawk to land a hundred yards beyond where the first one had. They didn't want to come in the same way to throw off the insurgents. That meant Ann and her men had to cross a narrow ledge along the ridge to get to the landing zone. They'd be sitting ducks for a sniper, but it couldn't be helped.

Ready? she signed to the others. Using sign language was as natural to Ann as breathing. She'd learned it as a child and it was a very effective way to communicate with her men when in situations where they couldn't hear each other or were too far away to talk safely. The first team she'd commanded had balked at learning the simple signs, but after an especially harrowing mission, they'd finally seen the benefits. From there on out, Ann had taken it upon herself to teach everyone under her command as much sign language as she could.

Mack and Gabe signaled back that they were ready, and Bell agreed from next to her.

"Thirty seconds," Bell warned a minute later.

"Go!" Ann signed to Mack and Gabe. As she and Bell laid down cover fire, the other two men scrambled up and headed across the narrow ledge. Ann held her breath until they were across. She saw Gabe give her the all clear.

"Your turn," she told Bell. "I'll cover you and when you get to the other side, you do the same."

She could see the hesitation in his eyes, but Ann hardened her voice. "Go," she ordered.

The sergeant nodded and headed for the ledge. The communication pack over his head and shoulder was bulky and he couldn't move as fast as his teammates.

Ann saw a sniper lie down and aim at Bell.

"Oh, hell no," she muttered as she took aim herself. As Mack and Gabe did their best to keep Wakil's men from hitting their teammate, Ann took a deep breath, then pulled the trigger of her own weapon.

Swamped with relief when she managed to take out the sniper before he could get a shot off, Ann readied herself to cross the narrow ledge. She could hear the Blackhawk coming in fast and hard in the distance. She didn't have much time.

As she stood up to run across the ledge, the unmistakable sound of an RPG being fired registered.

Between one second and the next, the rocket-propelled grenade hit dead center on the ledge she'd been about to cross. If she'd left five seconds earlier, she would've been blown to bits along with the side of the mountain.

Swearing, she heard the soldiers in the chopper firing their own RPG back at the insurgents. When the dust cleared enough, Ann saw that there was no way to join her teammates. There was literally a hole in the side of the mountain, cutting her off from them and the rescue chopper.

Clenching her jaw, Ann watched as Gabe, Mack, and Bell practically threw themselves into the opening of the helicopter. She saw Mack turn toward her before he signed.

What he was proposing wasn't likely to work, but she literally had no other choice. It was take a chance or be killed. And Ann wasn't ready to die.

She signed her understanding back and took a deep breath. She might not be ready to die, but death didn't take a person's hopes and dreams into consideration.

Ann lifted her weapon over her head and dropped it to the ground. She unstrapped her helmet and wiped more blood from her field of vision. She took off anything that might hinder her range of motion or weigh her down. She didn't worry about leaving her gear behind for the insurgents to recover. A few weapons wouldn't help their cause one way or another.

Keeping her eyes on the helicopter, she saw it begin to fly away, then held her breath as it made a sharp turn, laying down suppression fire as it came roaring back toward where she was standing.

Two soldiers leaned out of the open door and held out their hands.

Thirty feet. Twenty-five. Twenty feet. Fifteen feet. Ten. This was it.

The pilot had gotten the chopper as close to the edge where she was standing as he could. The ten feet seemed more like a hundred, but Annie didn't even hesitate. She'd been jumping and climbing on obstacle courses for as long as she could remember. This was a piece of cake.

Ann had room to take three running steps before she was flying through the air. Her arms outstretched. Her eyes glued to the hands reaching for her.

Everything else faded. The gunshots. The yelling. The sound of the helicopter.

For a split second she didn't think she was going to make it. That she would fall two feet short of her goal. But unlike any of the obstacle courses she'd gone through in the past, if she fell, it would be to her death.

It was only seconds, but it seemed like an eternity before she felt herself slam against the chopper. The pain was immense, but Ann barely registered it as her body began to slip backward. Scrambling for purchase, her legs dangling over the edge of the opening, Ann felt a split second of panic before her arms were caught in iron-tight grips.

She was dragged onboard by the two soldiers at the door even as the chopper banked and accelerated, hauling ass out of the valley.

Taking a deep breath, and regretting it as her cracked ribs made themselves known, Ann looked up, meeting the gazes of her teammates.

"Holy shit, Fletcher!" Bell breathed.

"I don't think I've ever seen anything like that before," Gabe said.

"Balls of steel," Mack said with a shake of his head.

"You all right, Captain?" one of the men who'd hauled her onboard asked.

"Peachy," she told him.

"Hang on!" the pilot yelled as the chopper tilted suddenly to the right.

Ann closed her eyes. She knew she should get up and help however she could. But at the moment, she was too relieved to be alive. That had been close. Too close. She hadn't had much chance to think about anything other than surviving for the last six hours, but in that moment, it all came crashing down.

She had to keep it together, but all she could think about was how close she'd come to losing *everything*.

Including a future with the man she loved.

For the first time ever, doubts about what she was doing with her life struck her—hard.

For as long as she could remember, Annie had wanted to serve her country. To make a difference like her dad had. Like his Delta Force team had done. She wanted to save lives, not take them, although she understood that being a part of an elite Special Forces team like the Green Berets meant she'd occasionally have to kill the enemy.

She wanted to prove to her father, all her honorary uncles, and to herself that she could do this. Wanted to make them proud.

But as she lay on the floor of the chopper after literally making a once-in-a-lifetime jump, Ann suddenly couldn't help but wonder what in the hell she was doing. Was this really what she wanted to do for the next fifteen or more years? Was this how she potentially wanted to die? Broken and bleeding thousands of miles from those she loved? If she died on a mission, no one would know exactly what happened. It was a fact of life for a Special Forces soldier.

Confusion muddled her brain. This was what being a Green Beret was all about. Taking risks to keep the world safe from dictators and terrorists who wanted to bring harm to innocents. But was she really making a difference? Even if they'd killed Wakil, there would be someone ready and willing to take his place. Wars had been fought since the dawn of time...was anything she was doing really that important in the grand scheme of things?

Her father and his team wouldn't be any less proud if she *wasn't* putting her life on the line. She knew that, intellectually. But that didn't ease the sense of anxiety at just the thought of letting them down.

She hated the foreign feelings coursing through her body, but she couldn't stop them.

Something had changed on that ridge, and she wasn't sure exactly what to make of it. All she knew was that the job she'd spent her entire life fighting for the right to have...suddenly didn't look quite so appealing anymore.

She was twenty-seven years old, but she felt decades older. She'd seen more than her fair share of death, destruction, and discrimination in her time in the Army. Her body hurt way more than someone her age should because of the abuse she'd heaped on it over the years. With every mission, the chance that she'd be permanently disabled from a bullet increased. Or she could be taken captive or even killed. It was the idea of the latter that made her inhale sharply. She couldn't imagine the pain her loved ones would experience if that happened.

With blood oozing down the side of her face from the cut over her eye, and each breath feeling as if she was being stabbed in the chest because of what had to be broken ribs, Ann closed her eyes and pictured the one person she wanted to see more than anyone else in the world. The man who made her feel safe. Who she fought to return to after every mission. The man she'd loved since she was seven years old.

Frankie.

CHAPTER TWO

Frankie Sanders paced his and Annie's small rental house nervously. It was the middle of the night, but he couldn't shake his unease. Annie had said she would get in touch with him after she got back from her recon mission. That had been over a day ago.

He knew communication when she was deployed was iffy, but for some reason, he had a bad feeling about this.

There wasn't a minute that went by when Annie was deployed that Frankie didn't worry about her. He was well aware she was a damn good soldier, but that didn't mean he didn't stress about where she was and what she was doing when she was gone.

Frankie had loved Annie since he was a kid. She'd been his rock, his biggest cheerleader for his entire life. There wasn't one birthday he could remember when she hadn't called. There wasn't one holiday when he didn't get to see her smiling face on his iPad. She was his first everything. Crush, love, kiss.

They'd even lost their virginity with each other.

Frankie had invited Annie out to California to attend his senior prom, and amazingly, her dad and his had both agreed. They'd gone to the dance, had taken some pictures, danced to one song, then he'd taken her to the hotel room he'd secretly rented for the night. He'd made everything as romantic as he could, including chocolate-covered strawberries, three dozen roses, bubble bath, and he'd even brought candles, though they were illegal to use in the hotel.

Instead of being nervous, Frankie had been relaxed and eager to make Annie's first sexual experience as beautiful as he could. They'd laughed that night, both a little unsure, but so much in love that a little awkwardness didn't faze either of them. He hadn't been able to hold her all night as he'd dreamed about doing, as they had a two o'clock curfew, but it was a night neither of them would ever forget.

It was just one of the hundreds of good memories he had of his fiancée. Being with Annie was easy. She accepted him exactly how he was, and he never laughed as much as he did when he was with her.

The day he asked her to marry him was one of the best in his life. They were no closer to their vows now than they were then, but Frankie didn't care how long he had to wait to make Annie his wife. She was worth waiting for.

He was as proud of Annie as he could be, but that didn't mean the anxiety he felt when she was gone lessened one iota. Her job was dangerous and there was always a chance he could lose her. So not hearing from her when she said she'd call meant Frankie couldn't sleep.

There could be a million reasons why she hadn't called.

No cell service. No Wi-Fi. Whatever mission she'd been on ran longer than expected. She was in meetings.

But the reason keeping him awake was the one he dreaded the most.

His phone vibrated in his hand, and Frankie glanced at it. He didn't recognize the number, but didn't hesitate to answer.

"Hello?"

"It's me."

Every muscle in Frankie's body seemed to relax at hearing Annie's voice. "Are you all right?"

"Yeah." She sounded tired.

"I was worried," Frankie told her.

"I know, and I'm sorry. I'm so damn sorry." Annie's voice hitched—and Frankie's breath froze.

He could count on one hand the number of times he'd seen Annie cry. She wasn't a crier. Much like her mother, she straightened her shoulders and carried on no matter what was going on in her life. He hated that he wasn't there with her. That he couldn't see her. When she was deployed, they couldn't FaceTime, were restricted by the functionality of the satellite phone she carried with her to communicate.

"Don't be sorry," he told her firmly. "I'm good. Everything here is fine. You just need to take care of yourself and come home to me."

"Well, the good news is that I'll be home sooner than I thought."

"That's great, baby. When?"

"Probably four days or so. We need to make a detour to Germany before heading home."

"Annie?" he said, his muscles tensing all over again. He knew what that meant. The base in Germany had a full-fledged hospital, and was the first place many soldiers were flown when they'd been injured in combat while abroad.

Frankie heard her inhale deeply. "Some of my guys are hurt. We're all being flown to Germany as a team to be assessed, then those of us who are cleared will be headed home."

"But *you're* okay?" Frankie asked.

"A few broken ribs and a nasty cut on my head," Annie said.

Frankie appreciated her honesty, even as he felt sick inside. He hated when Annie got hurt while on a mission. He knew it was a potential consequence of her job, but he couldn't help worrying about her being killed. He couldn't protect her. She wouldn't want him to protect her...but God, did he want to.

"I love you," he said softly.

"Not as much as I love you," she returned. "How're things there? Have you gotten any new clients?"

Frankie knew what she was doing. Trying to change the subject away from herself. He ached to hold her. To see for himself that she really was all right, wasn't downplaying her injuries to try to keep him from worrying. Which was impossible. He'd always worry about her. "They're good. No new clients, but remember that major I've been working with?"

"The one who lost his arm and hearing in the IED explosion six months ago?" Annie asked.

"Yeah. I think I'm finally getting through to him. We actually had a conversation via signing today."

"I knew you would," Annie told him, the pride easy to hear in her voice.

Frankie chuckled. "He's been having such a hard time accepting his disability. But this past weekend he was at the zoo with his grandchild, and he witnessed a kid slip and fall into one of the duck ponds. He saved the kid before anyone knew what was going on. I think that made him realize that even with his loss of hearing and his arm, he isn't helpless. That he can still make a difference even though he's not in the military anymore."

"That's good," Annie said softly.

Frankie heard someone yell for Annie in the background. "You need to go," he guessed.

"Yeah, I'm sorry."

"It's okay. I know how busy you are. Thank you for calling," Frankie said.

"I called as soon as I got back to the post and could get my phone," Annie told him. "My commander's on my ass to get over to the hospital."

"Jeez, Annie, you haven't seen a doctor for your injuries yet?" Frankie asked.

"No. I needed to hear your voice."

Again, he wished he could see her. She sounded off. Which wasn't like her at all. Typically after missions, she was hyped on adrenaline, or worried about the men on her team. Today she sounded...defeated. Which didn't sit well with Frankie. At all. "Well, you've heard it," he said sternly. "Now get your butt to the doctor."

She laughed, a sound that made him feel better. But only a little.

"Okay, okay, I'm going. I'll call when we get to

Germany and when I have a bit more of a concrete time-line on when I'll be back."

"Sounds good. I love you."

"Love you too."

"See you soon."

"Can't be soon enough for me," Annie said. "Bye."

"Bye."

Frankie clicked off the phone, but didn't move. He stood in the middle of the living room staring off into space for a long while.

Something was wrong.

Well, maybe not wrong...but definitely different.

He and Annie needed to have a talk. He hated knowing something was bothering her and not being able to do anything about it.

He thought about something his godfather, Cooper Nelson, had told him a long time ago when he'd first met Annie.

"Wait until the time is right. She might want to go to college, or fly to the moon, and you have to let her. Just let her know that you're right there beside her, cheering her on, whether you're literally beside her or thousands of miles across the country. When the time is right for you to claim your woman, you'll know it."

They'd been talking about Frankie wanting to marry Annie, and he'd taken Cooper's words to heart. Frankie would do anything for the woman. He'd stuck by her through junior high and high school, college and boot camp. They'd been stationed in three different cities in the years she'd been on active duty, and Frankie would live in a hundred more if it made Annie happy.

Tonight was the first inkling he'd gotten that she *wasn't*.

Maybe it was the adrenaline dump after an intense mission. Maybe it was the fact that she was hurting more from her injuries than she was letting on. But Frankie didn't think so.

He'd never heard Annie sound so...sad before.

When he'd asked her to marry him, Annie had warned him about how hard being a military spouse would be, especially married to someone in the Special Forces. She'd lived it with her mom being married to a Delta Force operative. Frankie had reassured her that he'd follow her to the ends of the Earth, that he'd love her unconditionally no matter what.

Even Fletch, her dad, had tried to warn him. Telling him that things would be tough.

Frankie hadn't cared. He'd understood and heard what everyone was telling him, but what they didn't understand was that he would do whatever it took to keep Annie happy. And being in the military, being part of a Special Forces team, had been her goal literally her entire life. Frankie wouldn't stand in the way of that, would encourage her and cheer her on every step of the way.

Taking a deep breath, Frankie moved toward their bedroom. He was exhausted, and he had to get up at his regular time in...Looking at his watch, he sighed. Three hours. It would be a long shift at the Veterans Affairs hospital tomorrow, but talking with Annie was worth any tiredness he'd have to struggle through.

Working with veterans who'd lost some or all of their hearing was a calling for Frankie. He'd always known what it was like to live as a deaf person in a hearing-centered world. And helping men and women transition to that world was something that gave him a deep sense of accomplishment.

Frankie's dad had arranged for him to get a cochlear implant when he was in the sixth grade. It had been a tough adjustment at first, and a very patient and understanding counselor at the hospital had helped him become accustomed to his new normal.

One of the best things he'd ever heard in his life was Annie's giggle the first time he'd called to tell her he could now hear.

Walking to the bathroom, Frankie brushed his teeth, then he slipped under the covers of the bed that seemed too big and empty without Annie. He took off the external microphone, sound processor, and transmitter system he wore behind his ear, which allowed the internal receiver and electrode system to receive signals, permitting him to hear. The magnet that held it in place made removing and attaching the device simple and easy.

Even now, it was still hard to believe this technology existed.

Closing his eyes at the blessed silence, Frankie rolled onto his back. He was grateful that he could hear. It made his life so much easier, but he couldn't deny there were times he was glad to be able to turn off his ears as well. His other senses took over when he couldn't hear and he could appreciate things differently than a hearing person.

Like the scent of Annie on the pillow under his head. He always switched pillows when she was gone, wanting to have something of her, even if it was just her scent, close while she was deployed. Even after she'd been gone for a week and a half, he could still smell her. Opening his eyes, Frankie could see the shoes Annie had toed off before she'd gotten in bed with him the night before her deployment, still sitting in the middle of the floor. He'd refused to move them, liking the sight of something so ordinary that reminded him of her.

Then there was her taste.

He shifted restlessly as his cock thickened. He really needed to get some sleep if he was going to function tomorrow, but he couldn't stop thinking about Annie, especially after that phone call. She was exuberant and had no problem taking charge in almost all aspects of her life, but in bed, she let him take the lead. She was almost shy, even after years together. Still blushing when he parted her legs and tasted her.

Turning onto his side, Frankie ignored his erection. He wasn't in the mood to masturbate. Not when he knew right that moment, Annie was seeing a doctor because she was hurt.

A few days and he'd get to see for himself that she was all right. That she was safe.

He took each deployment as it came. He couldn't think about the future. About where she might be sent and what she might be doing. For now, he was relieved that she'd made it through one more mission. He'd love and support her until she was deployed again.

She'd never know just how much he worried about her while she was gone. He never wanted to be a burden, so he'd get through each day as it came, smiling and supporting the only woman he'd ever love.

CHAPTER THREE

Annie's homecomings weren't like those for other soldiers. There were no parades, no huge crowds lined up to welcome the returning heroes. Most of the time, no one even knew the soldiers getting off the plane at the military airfield when Special Forces came back from a top-secret mission that could've saved dozens, hundreds, or thousands of lives.

Annie wasn't bitter about that. She'd known how things would work when she'd signed up to become a Green Beret. Yet somehow, every time she'd returned home from overseas, Frankie had been there. Even when she didn't give him specifics about her arrival time, he always knew. She suspected her dad's old friend Tex was involved in passing along the intel about her return. But she'd never asked Frankie, and he'd never volunteered the information. She just loved that he was always waiting for her. He was her reward for making it through each deployment.

Today was no different.

Annie walked across the tarmac toward the small building that housed the administrative offices for the airfield. She'd never been so glad to get home. She was still feeling off-kilter and she didn't know why. This mission wasn't all that different from a lot of the others she'd been on. This wasn't the first close call she'd had and it probably wouldn't be the last.

So why did she feel such a sense of dread weighing her down?

She knew it had everything to do with her thoughts on that helicopter, after her extraction. The thoughts that had dogged her ever since.

When she caught a glimpse of Frankie standing outside waiting for her, the darkness in her soul seemed to lighten. Moving slowly so as not to tweak her ribs, Annie returned the salutes she received from lower-ranking soldiers as she headed for the exit.

"Welcome home," said the man she loved more than life itself.

Annie walked straight into his embrace, snuggling into him as if it had been years since she'd seen him. Burying her face in the skin of his neck, she inhaled deeply, needing to get his woodsy, musky scent in her nose. God, she'd missed this. Missed *him*.

His arms closed around her carefully, as if he remembered hugging her tightly would hurt. Of course he remembered. Frankie was the most considerate man she'd ever met in her life.

"I missed you," Annie mumbled.

"No more than I missed you," he returned.

The comfort in the familiarity of their banter soothed

Annie. She lifted her head and Frankie reached for her duffle bag. She let him take it from her and wrapped an arm around his waist as he turned them to head for the parking lot.

Frankie wasn't a man of many words. He let his actions speak for him. He'd admitted more than once that he was self-conscious about the way he sounded when he spoke. Because he hadn't heard sound for years while growing up, his words weren't always fully formed, sometimes pronounced wrong, and his voice somewhat monotone. But Annie didn't care. To her, he was simply Frankie.

Lifting her free hand, she signed, "All good?"

Frankie nodded. His hands were full, one around her waist and the other holding her bag, so he responded out loud. "Everything's fine. I didn't burn the house down, got the lawn mowed, and even went to the grocery store this morning."

Annie chuckled. Of course Frankie would keep things running smoothly in her absence. He'd been doing it for years. He'd even had to oversee their move from Colorado to Kentucky alone, when she'd been unexpectedly deployed right before the movers arrived to pack up their stuff.

Guilt hit her once more. Her life in the Army wasn't anything like her mom and dad's had been. Most of Fletch's career, he'd been stationed in Texas. She hadn't had to move even once after her mom and Fletch had gotten married. Six or so years in, and she and Frankie had already moved three times.

"Stop," Frankie ordered.

Surprised, Annie looked up at him. "Stop what?" she asked.

"Thinking so hard. I don't like seeing you so...worried."

Annie took a deep breath. The last thing she wanted was to put more of a burden on Frankie than she already had.

"And stop that too," Frankie said.

Annie shook her head and smiled up at him.

"You're home. We're together. I made a huge batch of green chile stew yesterday because I know it's your favorite. We're gonna relax. Then we'll talk, you'll tell me what you can about your mission to get it off your chest. I'll examine you from head to toe to see for myself where you were hurt, then we'll go to bed and sleep the night through."

"You know me so well," Annie told him as they approached his truck.

"Yup. Just like you know me."

After putting her bag in the back, Frankie pressed her against the vehicle, his eyes going to the cut on her head. Annie had left off the bandage that morning because it was bothering her. Making the wound itch. She'd gotten off easy with three stitches, but the bruising on her forehead was pretty gnarly.

Frankie lifted a hand and gently brushed his fingers over the injury. He switched to signing instead of speaking and said, *Do you have a headache? Is the light bothering you?*

I'm okay, Annie signed back. *Promise.*

Then Frankie leaned forward and kissed the bruise. His lips were as soft as butterfly wings against her skin.

Feeling on the verge of tears, Annie pressed herself

against him once more, wanting to hide her vulnerability. She was always happy to be home, but today, she was feeling her mortality more than ever before. She was so damn relieved to be alive and with Frankie that it was almost overwhelming.

As if he knew how on edge she was, Frankie didn't press her to talk. He simply gathered her against him and held her. His grip was semi-painful, but Annie ignored the twinge. She needed this. Needed him.

"Come on," Frankie said after a minute. "I'm dying out here. The humidity today is around eighty-two percent and unlike you, I melt in the heat."

Annie grinned, relieved the funk she'd been feeling finally seemed to be dissipating. Frankie did that for her. He always had.

"Well, let's get you home before you're nothing but a pile of sweat with eyes then," she teased.

When he didn't immediately move to get in the truck, Annie frowned. "Frankie?"

"I love you," he said. "So much, you don't even know."

"I *do* know," she insisted. "Because I love you the same way."

Frankie nodded. "Come on. Have you called your dad?"

"No. I'll do it later."

"Okay. But don't wait too long. You know Tex'll have told him you're home by now."

It was just one more reason Annie suspected Frankie and Tex were closer than she probably knew. He threw the former SEAL's name around way too often for them *not* to be talking on a semi-regular basis. Annie knew she should probably be more irritated that the man was quite the busybody in her life, but she couldn't. She loved Tex as much as she did her dad's former teammates. Ghost, Coach, Hollywood, Beatle, Blade, Truck, and even Fish and Chase, were all her unofficial uncles and pain-in-the-butt brothers. They were overprotective and meddlesome, but she knew they behaved that way out of love.

If Tex watching over her gave comfort to everyone she cared about, she was all right with that. Besides, if there was anyone she'd want at her back, it was Tex. He'd proven time after time that he had the connections to get shit done.

"I know," she told Frankie. "I'll call Dad after we eat."

Frankie nodded.

When they were on their way back to the house, Annie asked, "Is my dad still giving you shit about making an honest woman out of me?"

Frankie glanced over at her before turning his attention back to the road. "No. Why? Is he giving *you* shit about not having set a date for our wedding? If he is, I'll talk to him and tell him to back off."

Annie stared at Frankie as he drove. He'd been a gangly teenager, but had definitely grown into a very good-looking man. His dark hair was a bit too long on top, and he had a five o'clock shadow. He was wearing a gray-shirt with short sleeves that showed off his toned and muscular biceps. His stomach was flat and he had a six-pack set of abs from regular workouts. His nose was slightly crooked from falling off his bike when he was in middle school, when he broke it. At the moment, his brows were drawn down in consternation, as if even the thought of her dad giving her grief annoyed him.

Annie had never been the kind of woman who needed or wanted a man to stand up for her. She was perfectly capable of holding her own against anyone who had a beef with her. She didn't hesitate to interject herself into situations where someone else was being picked on or harassed either. But knowing that this man—this amazing, wonderful, hot-as-hell man—was irritated on her behalf, made butterflies swirl in her belly.

"It's nothing I can't handle," she told Frankie.

"Seriously, Annie. If he's been on your case, I'll talk to him. When we do or don't get married isn't any of his business. We'll do it when the time is right for us both. And if that takes twenty more years—or even if it never happens—that doesn't mean we love each other any less."

"You don't want to get married?" Annie asked in surprise.

"I didn't say that. I've known since I was seven years old that I want to marry you, Annie. There's nothing I want more than to tie the knot in front of our friends and families. But I will *never* rush you into anything you don't want or aren't ready for."

"It's not that I don't want to marry you," Annie protested.

"I know, baby. I get it. You have so many responsibilities and goals, and people count on you to be there when they need them. It's fine. As I said, I have no problem waiting as long as it takes. You're it for me. There will never be another woman. Ever. So if your dad is giving you shit, I'll tell him to knock it off."

Annie snorted. "You'll tell Fletch to knock it off?" she asked skeptically.

"Okay, maybe not in those exact words," Frankie said with a grin. "He wouldn't take very kindly to that. Would probably challenge me to a duel in the backyard or something."

"He's not that bad," Annie insisted.

"Riiight," Frankie said, drawing out the word. "When I went to him for permission to ask you to marry me, he stared at me so intensely, I swear I thought he was gonna explode. Then he proceeded to give me an hour-long lecture about how if I ever made you cry, or hurt one hair on your head, he and his friends would make me disappear so thoroughly, no one would ever find any evidence of my existence...and certainly wouldn't ever find anything to prove that they'd done it."

Annie laughed. She'd heard this story so many times already, and each time Frankie told it, he embellished more and more. In truth, her mom had told her Fletch cried and agreed immediately. *Then* he'd warned Frankie that if he hurt his baby girl, he knew ten different ways to make a body disappear without a trace.

Reaching out, Annie put her hand on Frankie's thigh. She felt his muscle tighten...and just like that, desire rose within her. Only this man had ever made her feel that way. As if he didn't touch her, she'd die. Of course, with her broken ribs, making love would be difficult. And Frankie always seemed to know when she was hiding something from him, including pain.

"I want to marry you," she told him seriously.

"I know."

"I just...my mom's gonna want this huge shindig. And there are so many people we'll have to invite. It's gonna be a mad house, and my commander has been great about giving me time off, but it all seems so overwhelming."

"Say the word and we can go to Vegas," Frankie said.

Annie couldn't help but hear the longing in his voice. It was one more thing she felt guilty about.

She'd never told him the *real* reason why she'd put off marrying Frankie for so long. It wasn't that she didn't love him. She did. But early in her Army career, she'd overheard a general talking about her with another high-ranking officer. He'd been impressed with her enthusiasm and dedication, but then he'd said, *"I'm sure she'll run off and get married though, ruining her career. She'll want to pop out babies, and she'll get fat and out of shape. It's a shame, really, as I could see Lieutenant Fletcher rising up in the ranks if she devoted herself to her career."*

His words were insulting, derogatory, and discriminatory. They'd disgusted Annie—yet she'd never been able to shake them. The words had soaked into her psyche like an invasive virus.

She'd worked harder than those around her to prove to that general and everyone else that she wasn't like other women. She was serious about her career, about being the best Green Beret the Army had ever seen. She shouldn't give two fucks what other people thought about her...but to her shame, she did.

And now, three years had gone by since Frankie had asked her to marry him, and she'd said yes, and they still hadn't done the deed.

Frankie reached down and intertwined his fingers with hers. "But tonight, we aren't going anywhere," he said lightly. "We're gonna eat, you'll call your dad to let him know you're home, then you're gonna let me baby you a bit. One day at a time, right?"

"Right," she agreed. They'd talked about this years ago, when they'd moved to her first duty station. He'd found a job with the VA and it had served him well over their several moves, allowing him to keep his job, just working for a different hospital in each new location. He never complained. Simply took each obstacle they encountered with a grace and dignity that she admired.

"Close your eyes and relax," Frankie ordered.

Smiling, Annie squeezed his hand and did just that. She was safe with Frankie, she knew that down to her toes. Some of the stress that had built up within her over the least week eked away. Frankie was her safe harbor. She could be her real self with him. He was her biggest supporter.

Annie had a lot of decisions she knew she needed to make, but for now, she was home. She was alive. And she was with the most amazing man in the world. Everything else could wait.

Later that night—much later—Frankie lay in bed next to Annie, watching her sleep, and could finally let down his guard. When he'd first gotten a glimpse of her, he'd nearly fallen to his knees. She had a bruise that covered her entire forehead. It was still in the purple and red stage, meaning it was fairly fresh. The stitches in her brow didn't bother him nearly as much as that bruise did.

After dinner, and while she was reassuring her dad that

she was truly all right, he'd gone upstairs and run a hot bath for Annie. She'd always loved long, scalding soaks, and he couldn't think of a better welcome home than a relaxing bubble bath.

That's when he'd gotten a look at her torso. There was a deep purple bruise in a line across her chest, right beneath her breasts. She'd explained that it had come from hitting the edge of the helicopter she'd jumped into. She'd downplayed the incident, but Frankie knew what she was describing had been ten times scarier in reality.

He also knew without her having to admit it that she'd come close to dying on the side of whatever mountain she'd been on.

That bruise scared him to death. It looked painful as hell, and her broken ribs indicated just how hard she'd hit when she'd landed.

Frankie wouldn't insist Annie quit doing what she loved. She'd worked her ass off to get to where she was, in charge of her own Green Beret team. And she was obviously damn good at it. But if she gave him the slightest indication that she wanted to do something different with her life, he'd encourage her without reservations.

A little bit of Frankie died inside every time she came back to him bruised and battered.

He wasn't a very dominant person in general. With his disability and the way he was made fun of while growing up, he'd learned to fade into the background. But that didn't mean that he wouldn't protect Annie with everything he had in him. She was literally the only person who'd never judged him. From the first moment they'd met, she hadn't hesitated to befriend him and do her best to learn to communicate. No one else had ever done that. He was one hundred percent loyal to her. If he could, he'd use his bare hands to kill anyone who dared try to hurt her. She meant that much to him.

But at the moment, Frankie felt helpless. He could see Annie was struggling with something she wasn't ready to talk about. He would give her as much time and space as she needed to work through whatever it was. He had no doubt she'd eventually talk to him. In the meantime, he'd do what he'd always done—make sure she knew how much he loved her. It wasn't exactly a hardship.

Making love was out of the question for at least a few weeks until her ribs healed. He knew his Annie. She'd pretend she wasn't hurting, even if she was screaming in pain inside. So it would be up to him to be strong enough not to give in to their desire. It wouldn't be easy, but Frankie wouldn't hurt her. Not ever.

Reaching out, he put his palm over the bruise on Annie's chest. He gently rubbed his thumb back and forth on her sleep shirt, as if that could erase the horridness underneath the cloth.

"Frankie?" she mumbled.

He'd already taken off the speech processor component of his hearing device but could read her lips easily. "Shhhh," he murmured. "Go to sleep."

She shifted as if to roll toward him, but winced in pain at the movement.

Frankie moved his hand to her belly and pressed down lightly. "Stay still, love."

She nodded, then reached for his hand. She covered it

with her own and sighed in contentment as she fell asleep once more.

Frankie wasn't sure how long he lay awake watching his fiancée sleep, but eventually he couldn't keep his eyes open any longer. Moving closer so he'd feel if she got restless in the middle of the night and needed another painkiller, Frankie eventually fell asleep.

CHAPTER FOUR

"Are you as excited as I am for this month of leave?" Annie asked Frankie a few weeks later, when they were on a plane headed for Texas.

"Yes," Frankie said simply.

The bruise on Annie's forehead had disappeared and the scar over her eye would eventually fade so it wasn't noticeable at all. The guys on her Green Beret team were all in various stages of healing. Green and Bell wouldn't be back. Their injuries were too intensive for them to be able to be on the teams anymore. Shef was iffy, and regardless, he and Mack were being moved to another duty station, and thus another team.

Annie wasn't as close with her team as her dad had been with his, because the Army hadn't given her a chance to have that super-close bond. They kept moving her, or members of her team, to different stations.

Her own reenlistment date was quickly approaching. Annie had completed her initial six-year commitment—and was seriously considering calling it quits.

Instead of dissipating, those feelings on the helicopter had stayed with her for weeks, only getting stronger. Reminding her of what could happen the next time she was deployed. How she might not be so lucky again. But every time she thought about bringing it up with Frankie or her dad, panic and dread set in. Especially where Frankie was concerned. He'd given up so much for her to fulfill her dream. How could she just up and quit now?

Though, the fact that she was looking forward to this vacation as much as she was...it made her more and more certain that she didn't want to re-up. She couldn't remember when they'd spent an entire month together without having to worry about the phone ringing and her being called up for a mission.

They were headed to Killeen first, where Annie's brother Doug was graduating from high school. Even Ethan was coming home from the University of Boulder in Colorado for the occasion. It had been a long time since the entire family had been together. Her three brothers were crazy busy, even John, who was thirteen, seemed to be gone more than he was home.

After the graduation ceremony, she and Frankie were headed out on the trip of a lifetime, spending two weeks on a four-masted sailboat. It was a large ship, holding around sixty guests and thirty crew. The itinerary was taking them to some of the smaller islands in the Caribbean, many of which Annie had never heard of.

This was more Frankie's dream vacation than Annie's, as he was somewhat of a boat nut. There weren't many of the huge sailboats still operating today, and she knew he couldn't wait to watch the crew put up and take in the sails each day. They did it the old fashioned way, climbing up the masts and unfurling the sails by hand.

Because Annie worked so much, and rarely took time off, they had plenty of money saved up. Enough to splurge on the trip.

"What are you thinking about so hard?" Frankie asked.

Annie glanced at him. Her man looked exceptionally good today. He was wearing a pair of khaki pants and a polo shirt, filling out both perfectly. He'd finally gotten a haircut, and she'd noticed various women in the airport checking him out. Sometimes Annie had to pinch herself that he was hers. She knew she was hardly hideous, but she was a little too muscular, too assertive, cared too little about wearing makeup and girly clothes to appeal to a vast majority of the men she met. Frankie didn't give a damn about any of that. He loved her exactly as she was.

"I'm just so ready for this vacation," she told him.

Frankie took her hand in his and lifted it to his lips, kissing the back. "Me too. You gonna talk to your dad about your reenlistment?"

Annie blinked in surprise, then quickly tried to cover her reaction. "Why would I do that?"

Frankie looked at her with such gentleness and love, it made Annie want to weep.

"Because you're stressed out. And because you're thinking about not re-upping."

This time, she was genuinely shocked. She hadn't said a word to Frankie about her misgivings. Though she supposed she shouldn't be surprised that he could read her so well.

She sighed. "Is it that obvious?" she asked softly.

"Only to me. Annie, I know you. I know when you're happy and when you're mad. I know when you're stressed out and when you're sad. I haven't said anything because I wanted to give you space to work things out on your own, and I hoped you'd come to me to discuss it when you were ready. But ever since you got back from your last mission, you've been on edge. Every time the phone rings, you jump, and your team being broken up has affected you more than it has in the past."

Annie stared at Frankie. She'd never been able to keep anything from this man. He'd always been completely in tune with how she was feeling. And clearly, her mood had affected him too. It was one more thing that made her feel guilty.

"I just...I've always wanted to be in the Army. In the Special Forces. I've worked my ass off to get here, and it feels awful to turn my back on it," she said after a long moment.

"You aren't seven anymore. Or thirteen. Or eighteen. Or even twenty-five. People change, Annie. Our wants and desires change. There's nothing wrong with you wanting something different. What *do* you want?"

Annie met Frankie's gaze head on. "I want to come home to you every day. I want to laugh more. And I don't want to die in some desert somewhere. I don't want you to have to go through that. I'm proud of what I've accomplished, but it just feels as if life is passing me by."

It felt good to finally admit her innermost thoughts. She should've done this before now. Sitting in an airplane wasn't exactly the best place for super-intense confessions, but when she looked into Frankie's dark eyes, she couldn't shut up.

"There's a lot I love about the Army. Always have, always will. There's a comradery that I can't fully explain to anyone who hasn't experienced it. I like the discipline as well. There's comfort in routine, if that makes sense. Knowing I'm doing my part to keep people safe fulfills something deep inside me. I actually enjoy crawling in the dirt and seeing the surprise on people's faces when they realize I'm a woman...and kicking their ass. I'm proud of what I've accomplished and every time I put on my uniform, it makes me want to be a better person."

"But?" Frankie asked.

Annie sighed. "I want to be Mrs. Annie Sanders," she said softly. "I want to find a place to settle down and know we'll be there for longer than two years. I don't have any friends, Frankie. I mean, the guys I work with on post are great, but I have no one to hang out with like my mom's circle. I want that. I want someone I can call to chat about nothing. To get drunk with every now and then. To gossip with. Right now, I can't see that happening as long as I'm at the mercy of the Army. And most of all, I want you to be able to do what *you* want. As long as I'm a Green Beret, you'll forever have to put your wants and desires after mine. I *hate* that."

Frankie reached out and put his hand behind her neck, pulling her into him until their foreheads were touching. "You want to know what *I* want, love?"

Annie nodded.

"I want *you* to be happy. I can always find a job with the

VA wherever the Army sends you, so that's not an issue. I don't care where I am, as long as it's with you."

Annie took a deep breath to keep from bursting into tears. "I feel the same, but lately, we haven't been able to spend that much time together. I hate it, Frankie. I spent my entire childhood missing you, and even though we're living together now, I'm gone more than I'm home. I don't want to resent the Army for that, but I'm starting to."

"What happened on that last mission?" Frankie asked.

Annie knew he wasn't asking about the specifics of the mission itself. But it was obvious something had changed for her. She never shared her close calls with Frankie, wanting to protect him from that aspect of her job. But he wasn't an idiot. He knew what she did wasn't exactly safe. He saw the aftermath of her injuries. And yet he still stood by her and was her biggest champion.

Frankie shifted, shoving up the arm rest between them and pulling Annie closer. He put his arm around her shoulder, and Annie snuggled into him as best she could in the uncomfortable airplane seat. It was easier to talk when she wasn't looking at him. And she had no doubt that had been his intention.

"We were ambushed. It was just the seven of us against who the hell knows how many bad guys with guns. We held them off for hours, but we were slowly being picked off one by one. By the time the helicopter came to extract us, we were all exhausted and injured. I started thinking about what I was doing. Why. If I'd died out there, no one would know the details. I'd just become another secret mission in a file somewhere, most of the information redacted. I'd miss out on growing old with you. On everything normal couples get to do. People might say, 'Oh that Annie Fletcher, she died doing what she loved.' But you know what?"

"What?"

"I'm not sure I love it so much anymore," Annie whispered, as if even saying the words out loud was somehow blasphemous. She hurried to add, "I'm not saying I want to start wearing a dress and makeup and heels every day, sitting behind a desk. But lying in the dirt, trying to kill people I know nothing about and who probably have families they love as much as I do...it doesn't hold the appeal it once did."

"What do you want to do then?" Frankie asked.

Annie closed her eyes. This was just one of the million and one reasons why she loved this man. He didn't try to talk her out of how she felt. He supported her with no reservations, no conditions. She wanted to do the same for him. She felt as if she'd been selfish for their entire relationship. He'd quit very good jobs to follow her around the country. He didn't have any friends either. She wanted stability for them both. Wanted what her parents had.

"I don't know," she admitted. "I'm not sure who Annie Fletcher is without the Army. I know I shouldn't care what other people think, but I can't help but feel as if I'd let so many people down if I got out. My dad brags about me all the time. Even to people like cashiers in the grocery store. He doesn't let any opportunity go by without informing someone who doesn't already know that I was one of the first females accepted into the Green Berets. The last thing I want is to see disappointment in the eyes of people I love the most."

"The people you love the most will continue to be proud of you, no matter what you might decide to do."

Annie took a deep breath. Deep down, she knew that, but it was hard to think about doing anything other than being a soldier.

"If you could do anything in the world, what would you want to do?" Frankie asked. "Be in charge of the soldiers going into battle? Sit on a beach somewhere with your feet in the sand and no responsibilities? Learn a foreign language and move to a different country and find a job? Don't think about it too hard, go with your gut. And heart."

Even though she'd claimed just a minute ago she didn't know what she wanted to do if she got out of the Army... that wasn't quite true. "I love being a medic," she said. "I like the prospect of healing people rather than killing them." Taking a deep breath, she said what she'd never had the guts to admit out loud before. "I think...I think I want to try to be a doctor."

"You want to change your MOS? You could see if the Army would send you to school. You could stay in and be a doctor at the same time," Frankie said.

Annie thought about that for a moment. It was a possibility, but she'd still be at the mercy of the government. They could send her anywhere, at any time, and she'd have no choice but to go. She wasn't sure that would make her any happier. She wanted to put down roots, which was extremely difficult while in the military.

"You'd be an amazing doctor," Frankie told her softly.

"It would mean going back to school," Annie said skeptically. "And probably just as much time away from home in the beginning, you know, long hours studying, and then a residency and all. It's ridiculous, really."

"It's not," Frankie said firmly. He lifted Annie's chin and forced her to meet his gaze. "You know how I know?"

"How?" Annie whispered.

"Because I hear the passion and excitement in your tone. You're never going to be happy with a sedentary job. You need the adrenaline. The excitement. The challenge. Which is another reason to get out of the Army now. You've said before that the time is coming when you'll be moved to a desk because of your rank. You won't be out in the field doing what you do best, you'll be stuck in the background."

"I know you're right, but med school costs a ton," Annie protested. "And I'll still be gone a lot."

"Here's the thing...I knew when we were in high school that I'd always fade into your background," Frankie said.

Annie opened her mouth to protest, but he went on, not letting her speak.

"And I'm okay with that. I don't like the limelight. You know that. I sound funny when I talk and it turns people off. That's their issue, not mine, but I'm much happier standing behind you, having your back, than being in front leading the way. I don't mind being Captain Fletcher's boyfriend, and I certainly won't mind being Doctor Sanders's husband.

"You have a gift, Annie. Everyone loves you. They can't help it. It's just who you are. I think you'd make an amazing doctor. You'll fight for your patients, and if you can't help them, you'll find someone who can. You won't rest until you discover what their issue is and fix it, instead

of just throwing drugs at the problem. I can tell you this—
if I was sick or hurt, I'd want you to be my doctor. Because
I know you'll do whatever it takes to make me well again. I
don't care what specialty you choose. I already know you'll
be the best in your field."

God. Annie didn't deserve this man. "You don't sound
funny," she told him.

Frankie smiled and shook his head in exasperation.
"*That's* what you heard out of all that?" he asked.

Annie shrugged. "I don't like it when you put yourself
down. You're incredible, Frankie. And anyone who can't
see that is an idiot."

"So...you gonna talk to your dad about all this?" he
asked, shifting the subject away from him, as he
always did.

Annie winced and snuggled back into Frankie's side. "I
don't want to let him down."

"You won't."

"You don't know my dad," Annie muttered.

But Frankie heard her. "I do," he insisted. "I've known
him for just about as long as you have. And yeah, I haven't
lived with him, but that man loves you more than anything
in this world. You're his little girl. His only daughter. His
sprite. He's bent over backward your entire life to make
sure you're happy."

"He's a legend," Annie protested. "His Delta Force
team is still talked about with awe. They had so many
successful missions and he lived and breathed the Army.
Hell, he still helps out on post, and he's not exactly young
anymore. I saw how proud he was when I accepted my
commission at my college graduation. I can't bear to see

the disappointment in his eyes when I tell him I want to get out."

"I think you're underestimating him," Frankie said.

"Maybe. Maybe not. And don't even get me started on the others. It would kill me to let Ghost and everyone else down. And Truck...God, I can't tell him. I think it was his idea all those years ago to get me that electric tank toy. I was a holy terror driving that thing around."

"I've seen the videos," Frankie said with a chuckle. "But again, I don't think they'll be disappointed in you. Not at all."

"Making the decision to get out scares the hell out of me. It's all I've ever known. I don't know for certain that I *do* want to get out. I mean, it's possible this last mission is just messing with my head. In a week, I'll probably look back at this conversation and be amazed I thought about quitting for even one second," she said with a small shrug.

"Or maybe you'll feel as if it was the best decision you ever made," Frankie countered.

"Maybe I'll just pretend I'm still in for the rest of my life. My dad and the others don't need to know," Annie joked.

She felt the chuckle rumble through Frankie's chest under her cheek. "Um, have you forgotten Tex?" he asked.

"Shit. Tex will know the second the paperwork gets filed, won't he?" Annie asked rhetorically. Of course he would. And he'd go straight to her dad to make sure she was all right. To find out what might be wrong.

"I'm sorry this has been weighing on you," Frankie said seriously. "But no matter what you decide, to re-up or to go to med school, or sit on a beach somewhere, I'll support you one hundred percent."

"I don't deserve you," Annie told him.

"Yeah, you do. We were meant for each other," he said simply.

He was right. They were. Everyone thought they'd grow out of their crush, especially since it started at age seven. Instead, their love had only grown stronger as they'd gotten older.

"I love you," Annie said.

"And I love you."

She looked up. "I want to get married."

She saw the spark of excitement—and relief?—in his eyes, and it nearly killed her. She'd done that. She hadn't meant to put him off forever, but her job kept getting in the way and the thought of tying him to her, then being killed, made her physically ill. She didn't want to hurt this man, but in putting off their wedding, she'd done just that.

"Any time. Any place. You know that," Frankie said.

"I'll talk to my mom."

He smiled. "Don't let her go crazy," he warned. "You know if she has her way, there will be a thousand people and she'll get Tex to invite the Queen of England or something."

Annie giggled. Frankie wasn't wrong. "I'm sorry I didn't talk to you about all this before. I mean, you have as much say in my decisions as I do, since they affect you just as much."

Frankie shook his head. "Don't be sorry. You needed to think things through on your own. You've always been that way. I just don't want you to ever be afraid of talking to me about anything. And you could never let me down. Ever. If you said you wanted to quit and become a circus clown, I'd be behind you one hundred percent. All I want, all I've ever wanted, is for you to be happy. And if the Army isn't doing that for you anymore, then you need to find something that does."

"I don't want to quit and become a circus clown," Annie said with a shiver.

"I know." He laughed. "You saw twenty minutes of the movie *It* and had to turn it off."

"Because it was *creepy*!" Annie insisted. "Give me a hundred insurgents with RPGs over a damn clown any day of the week. Frankie?"

"Yeah?"

"What do you want to do? What makes *you* happy? We've talked about me me me, but I don't want our relationship to only be about what I want."

"I want to do what I'm doing. Help others acclimate to hearing loss. To show them that their lives aren't over. That they can live a productive and fulfilling life. Love. Be loved. And I can do that from anywhere. As far as what makes me happy? You do. It's always been you, Annie."

His words melted her heart. Frankie was a good man. The best. And he was hers. He might not be a Special Forces commando. Might not have muscles upon muscles, but she knew if the shit hit the fan, he'd protect her with his life if he needed to. He'd be a rock and an asset, never a liability. Many people underestimated him because of how he sounded when he talked and because without the speech processor of the cochlear implant, he was completely deaf, but Annie knew better. He was mild mannered most of the time, but when provoked, her man was a force to be reckoned with.

Frankie kissed her forehead and she closed her eyes. She felt one hundred percent better now that she'd talked to him. She was still scared to talk to her dad...but for the first time, a spark of excitement welled up inside her. Becoming a doctor wouldn't be easy, but then again, neither was breaking into the ranks of the elite Green Berets.

She wasn't sure yet what she was going to do, but the anticipation and eagerness she felt about taking up a new challenge couldn't be ignored. She hadn't felt this way about her career in a long while. She could continue with the Army...but the fact of the matter was, she no longer felt a thrill when she got the call that she was being deployed.

Before she decided anything, she needed to talk to Fletch, despite how much that scared her. She wanted his opinion. She valued what he thought. Frankie was right; her dad loved her and wanted the best for her. He'd listen to whatever she had to say and give her his advice and thoughts. She hated for him to have even a second of disappointment in her, but if she didn't love her job anymore, could she really stay in it for the next fifteen years or more?

She didn't think so. Especially because her life, and the lives of the men and women under her command, depended on her committing one hundred percent. And she was no longer sure she could do that.

Annie wished she had the conviction and was as sure of herself as she'd been five years ago. Or ten. But as Frankie said...people changed. She just had to figure out if her current feelings about being a Green Beret were because of the close call on her last mission, or something deeper.

Taking a breath, Annie did her best to clear her mind. She had plenty of time to think about what she was going to do with the rest of her life. For now, she wanted to enjoy a well-earned vacation and look forward to seeing her family again.

CHAPTER FIVE

Frankie sat at the Fletchers' dinner table and smiled at the chaos. They'd all attended Doug's graduation ceremony that morning, and now they were having a family dinner before Doug headed out to celebrate with his friends for the evening. Tomorrow, the family was throwing a huge graduation party, and he knew from experience the amount of people there would be insane. It seemed that Fletch and Emily knew just about everyone.

It had taken a bit of getting used to for Frankie. It was just him and his dad for so long, joining this huge, crazy family had been a bit of a shock. He shouldn't have been too surprised. He'd seen how close military Special Forces teams could be through his godparents. Cooper and Kiera were tight with a Navy SEAL team out in California, and Frankie and his dad were frequently invited to hang out with everyone at beach parties.

At the moment, Annie's thirteen-year-old brother John was telling her about his last debate competition, where he came in second place overall.

"I'm not surprised," Annie teased. "You've always been an argumentative pain in the butt."

"I learned it all from you," he quipped.

"Will someone please pass the rolls?" Ethan asked.

Fletch grabbed the basket and handed it to his oldest son. Emily leaned over and put another spoonful of green beans on John's plate as he and Annie argued good-naturedly. Frankie saw Doug glancing at his phone and, after a minute or two, he asked, "May I be excused?"

Fletch wiped his mouth with a napkin. "You get enough to tide you over for tonight, son?"

"Yeah, Dad. Thanks."

"Curfew is one o'clock. I know you're a high school graduate and all, but that doesn't mean all rules end. Have fun. If you need me, call. I'll be up."

That was one of the things Frankie loved about Annie's dad. He was a hard-ass, there was no doubt. He expected his children to get good grades, make good decisions with their friends, and be good human beings, but he also knew they'd screw up. It was inevitable. And he made sure when that happened, each of them knew he'd have their backs, no matter what.

He was also impressed with the subtle reminder that Fletch would be waiting up for Doug, to ensure he met his curfew.

"Thanks, Dad. The guys and I are just going to hang out at Tom's house," Doug said.

"Isn't Julio having that huge graduation party tonight?" Ethan asked.

"Yeah, but we aren't really interested in going. Every-one's just gonna get drunk, and since literally everyone in town knows it's happening, the cops'll bust it before ten o'clock. Mark my words. Besides, Harley gave me the newest version of *This is War* that she's been working on, the one that doesn't come out for another two months. We want to see how fast we can conquer it."

"Good luck with that," Fletch said. "I hear it's the hardest version yet."

Doug's eyes lit up with the challenge. "We'll see about that," the teen said.

"Go," Fletch ordered. "But bring your plate to the kitchen and put it in the dishwasher first."

"And give your mother a kiss," Emily added.

Doug stood and picked up his plate, kissing his mom on the way to the kitchen.

"I'm done too, Dad. Can I be excused?" John asked.

"May I," Emily corrected.

"*May* I be excused?" John asked again. "My friends and I are working on that screenplay we're writing." He turned to Annie. "It's about a group of boys who have to save the world from an alien race that wants to take over and enslave all humans."

"Go," Fletch said with a chuckle.

"I think you need to throw a girl in the group," Annie told her brother.

John stuck out his tongue at his sister. "Why would we do that? Girls are annoying." Then he pushed back his chair and disappeared into the kitchen with his dishes.

"What about you, Ethan?" Emily asked. "You have big plans for the night?"

Ethan shrugged. "I'm gonna call my girlfriend, then go and hang out with Avi.

"How's he doing?" Annie asked.

Avi had been Ethan's best friend ever since they'd met in the tenth grade, when he'd moved to the US from India. He was literally the smartest person Frankie knew. He'd been a great influence on Ethan, and the two of them were still as close today as they were when they'd been in high school.

"He's good," Ethan said. "He's getting a second master's degree while he's working on his Doctorate. He said he needed a challenge."

Everyone chuckled.

"His parents have been trying to set him up with an Indian woman for years now, and he's fought it every step of the way. But he actually clicked with the last girl they introduced him to. He's talked to her on the computer every night for weeks. She's still back in India, and I think he's fallen in love," Ethan said.

"That's great. What's the problem?" Emily asked.

Ethan shrugged. "I think he's resisting because he doesn't believe in arranged marriages, even though they're still very common in his culture. And it's no secret that her parents have been talking to his about their children getting married."

"You want my advice?" Emily asked, not giving her son a chance to agree or disagree. "Tell him to forget about all that crap. If he and this woman have clicked, how they were introduced and why means nothing. It's not easy to find someone to connect with, so if he has, Avi should put aside the circumstances of their meeting and go for it."

Ethan grinned. "That's what I told him too."

"Good. He's coming to the party tomorrow, right?" Emily asked.

"Yeah. He says he wouldn't miss your pigs in a blanket."

Frankie burst out laughing, along with the rest of the Fletcher family. Avi was well known for his love of American kid foods. Chicken nuggets, French fries, pizza puffs, pretzel dogs, quesadillas, cheese sticks, mac and cheese, Chex mix...even s'mores. He might be twenty-two, but he ate like an eight-year-old. And since Annie's mom did her best to spoil everyone around her, Avi loved visiting.

"You staying over at his house tonight?" Fletch asked.

"Naw. I promised John I'd read over his screenplay in the morning. I shouldn't be too late," Ethan said.

"It's good to have you home for a while, son. Even if it's not as long as we'd like," Fletch said. Father and son smiled at each other before Ethan pushed back his chair and headed for the kitchen.

"Look at all this leftover food," Emily said on a sigh. "I remember when I literally couldn't feed those boys enough. They practically ate us out of house and home. And now they barely touch their dinner before they're up and off to hang with their friends or do something more interesting than keep their parents company."

Fletch reached out and pulled his wife closer, kissing her on the forehead. "Maybe if you hadn't made four tons of food, they could've made a dent in it," he teased.

"Whatever," Emily said with a roll of her eyes.

Frankie admired the relationship between Annie's parents. They were obviously completely devoted to each other and just as in love today as when they'd met over twenty years ago.

"Want to help me get all this put away, Annie?" Emily asked her daughter.

"Of course," she said immediately.

"Thanks. I also need to finish icing Doug's cake and get some more cookies in the oven."

"How did I know I'd get roped into helping you bake?" Annie said with a laugh.

"Because you know me," Emily told her with a smile.

Annie turned to Frankie. "You'll be okay?"

Before he could reassure her that of course he'd be fine, Fletch spoke up.

"What do you think I'm gonna do to him, sprite? Make him do pushups in the backyard? Take him to post and force him to run the obstacle course? Jeez, give your old man a break."

Annie giggled and went over to where Fletch was sitting. She leaned down and kissed him on the cheek. "Of course not. But you aren't above sitting him down and interrogating him about that new security system we put in a few months ago. You know, just to make sure it's *adequate*."

"Is it?" Fletch asked with a raise of his eyebrow.

Annie rolled her eyes at her dad and she looked so much like her mom, Frankie could only smile.

Emily Fletcher was a very good-looking woman. If Annie aged half as well as her mom, Frankie would be a lucky man. But honestly, he didn't care what Annie looked like, he just hoped she never lost her sass. She was proud of who she was and didn't care that she didn't conform to what many people thought a woman should look and act like. She wasn't afraid to get dirty, asked a million questions about something she wanted to understand better, rarely wore heels, and would rather spend her free time tromping around a jungle sweating her ass off than lounging by a pool or on a beach, working on her tan.

Annie had never put much stock in her looks. She'd said more than once that people could either like her for who she was on the inside, or get lost. If they looked down on her because she didn't wear makeup and preferred over-sized T-shirts and old holey jeans, then they weren't someone she wanted to get to know. Even now, her shoulder-length dirty-blonde hair was still in disarray from crawling under the back deck before dinner, just to get a look at a litter of kittens a stray cat had given birth to.

Frankie literally loved everything about this woman, including her positive attitude about life and the way she often acted before truly thinking about what she was doing. It scared him to death sometimes, but that was just who she was.

"Of course our security is top notch," Annie told her dad. "Tex recommended it, so you know it's the best."

Fletch merely smiled.

"Be nice, Daddy," Annie warned him. Then she headed for where Frankie was still sitting. She leaned down and kissed him on the lips. For years, it felt awkward to kiss Annie in front of her dad, given his high intimidation factor. When he never pulled out a weapon and threatened to kill him where he stood, Frankie had eventually relaxed his self-imposed moratorium on kissing or touching Annie in front of the man.

"Love you," Frankie said.

"Love you too," Annie echoed, then picked up as many

dishes as she could carry and, balancing them precariously, headed into the kitchen after her mom.

"How about we go to my office where it's more comfortable?" Fletch asked.

Frankie nodded. He'd been expecting this since he'd first caught Fletch staring at Annie with a pensive look on his face. He wasn't surprised the man had immediately realized something was bothering his daughter. Annie was stressed about whether to get out of the Army or not, and Frankie knew she would be until she talked with her dad and heard for herself that Fletch wouldn't be disappointed if she decided to do something different with her life.

He stood up and started to grab some of the dishes that were still on the table, but Fletch shook his head. "Leave them."

Frankie was surprised. Fletch was big on sharing the household chores, and he had trained his children to do the same. He'd heard the man say more than once that Emily wasn't their housekeeper and his kids needed to learn to take care of themselves, as their mom and dad wouldn't be there to clean up after them for the rest of their lives.

Noting Frankie's hesitance, Fletch said, "Em's gonna do her best to keep Annie occupied so we can talk, but I know my daughter, she's gonna want to check on us sooner rather than later, and I'd like to chat without her interrupting."

Frankie nodded and followed Fletch through the living room, down the hall, and into his office. He'd known the man almost his entire life. Had first met him when Frankie was in the first grade, and Cooper and Kiera had brought him to Texas to visit. That was when he'd fallen in love with Annie. He'd had plenty of conversations with Fletch over the years, including the one where he'd asked the man for permission to marry his daughter. He hadn't been nearly as nervous about that talk as he was right this second.

He liked Fletch. Respected him. But he absolutely would *not* break Annie's confidence. She needed to be the one to talk to her dad about her changing feelings for the Army, and what she wanted to do in the future. It wasn't Frankie's place to share her innermost thoughts. He'd do anything for her, even brave pissing off her dad by not saying a damn word about what was bothering his daughter. But he could do his best to smooth the road a bit.

Too bad he couldn't pretend his implant was malfunctioning. Fletch knew sign language as well as his daughter. Frankie had been blown away the first time her dad had actually spoken to him with his hands. Apparently he'd seen the writing on the wall as far as his daughter's love for Frankie, and had made it a priority to be able to communicate with him.

It was safe to say that Frankie liked everything about Fletch. He was protective, but not over the top about it. He was supportive, tough but fair, and his family's biggest champion. He could also be the scariest son-of-a-bitch in the world when someone or something threatened those he loved. He reminded Frankie a lot of Cooper, his godfather.

Frankie settled into one of the comfortable, oversized chairs in the room, as Fletch sat in another. He didn't sit behind the large imposing desk in the corner. Didn't try to put himself in a position of power over Frankie.

"I'm gonna cut to the chase," Fletch said. "Something's bothering Annie. And I'm not talking about her almost-healed ribs either. She seems...off-kilter. She's smiling, laughing, and saying all the right things, but I can tell that she's not quite herself. Is she stressed about going on vacation? I know how much she loves her job and hates to take time off."

"It's not the vacation," Frankie told Fletch honestly. "I mean, I know she's not as excited as I am to be on a sailboat, but she's looking forward to the time off. Her last mission was...hard." That was an understatement, but Frankie didn't know of another way to say it.

Fletch chuckled, but it wasn't a humorous sound. "It was a clusterfuck," he said with a shake of his head.

He wasn't surprised the man was aware of what had happened. He always knew more of the details about where his daughter had gone and what she'd done than Frankie. Perk of his previous job. But this time, it was the mission's impact on Annie's heart and mind, rather than her body, that mattered.

Fletch leaned forward and rested his elbows on his knees. "How come you two haven't gotten married?" he asked. "You've been engaged for over two years now."

Frankie blinked. It wasn't what he thought the man was going to ask. He thought he'd try to pry details out of him about whatever was bothering Annie. But he should've known Fletch would want to talk about this. He'd been excited and happy when Frankie had proposed to his daughter. Had expected them to be married by now. Hell, *Frankie* had expected them to be married by now.

"She's not ready," Frankie said simply.

Fletch's eyes narrowed. "You aren't just saying that to cover your ass, are you? I mean, if you've got cold feet, just admit it."

Frankie sat up straighter and gave Fletch a hard look. "I would marry your daughter tomorrow if she said the word. All I've ever wanted was to be with Annie. I've loved her for over twenty years. Cold feet?" He shook his head. "Not even close."

"Then why? Annie loves you. Why are you guys waiting?" Fletch asked, his brows furrowed in confusion.

Frankie sighed. "Honestly? I'm not completely sure. But I promised when I asked her to marry me that I wouldn't pressure her. When she's ready, she'll tell me. A ring and a piece of paper won't make a difference in my love for her. Won't make me act differently toward her."

"It'll help her career," Fletch said bluntly.

Frankie tensed. He was on thin ice talking about Annie's Army career, but he couldn't let that comment go. "The Army's different now than when you were in. No offense, but officers don't need to be married to be promoted."

"But it helps," Fletch insisted. "Look, I'm not saying I agree with it. It's bullshit. Attitudes have changed, yes. Look at Annie. Twenty years ago, she never would've been able to be a Green Beret. And to have a woman in charge of a Special Forces squad? No fucking way. But she's proven that she can handle it. That she's an asset and not a liability. That doesn't mean there aren't people out there who believe women should be in the background, shouldn't have high positions in the military, and should be married, barefoot, and pregnant. I'm just saying...it *could* help her career if she was married. And you two love each other, so I don't understand why you haven't just tied the knot already."

"I'd do anything for your daughter. Literally *anything*. You know that. And if she's not ready to get married, I'm not going to force her. I want to be a man she can rely on. Who will support and love her unconditionally. I'm okay with being a house husband. I'm okay with her saving the world while I stand at her side, or even behind her. What I'm *not* all right with is shoving her into some damn box society thinks she should be in. Being unmarried doesn't make me love her any less. When the time is right, we'll take that step. But if the time is never right, that's okay too. I'm not going anywhere."

Fletch stared at him for a long time, and Frankie didn't even blink. He wasn't the most assertive man. Didn't particularly like confrontation. But he'd go toe-to-toe with anyone who questioned Annie or her decisions. Including her father.

Finally, Fletch nodded reluctantly, his shoulders dropping a bit. "I just worry about her."

Frankie nodded. "I know."

"She's always been a damn-the-consequences kind of person. Has done what she wants, no matter what others think about it. It's gotten her in trouble a time or two, but mostly it's just made her stronger. She's a unique woman, and I'm so damn proud of her."

"She's scared of letting you down," Frankie blurted.

He frowned. "What?"

"You have no idea how much she looks up to you. You've been an amazing influence on her life and she doesn't want to disappoint you. In anything."

Fletch snorted. "That's impossible. She could never disappoint me. She might make decisions I wouldn't, but that doesn't mean that they aren't right for *her*. And even if I thought she'd made a wrong decision, I have no doubt she'd learn from any mistake, let it make her a better person, a better soldier and leader, in the long run. Is this about her getting married?" he asked, the confused look back on his face.

"No."

The two men stared at each other for a long moment. Then Fletch nodded. "Right. It seems I need to have a talk with my little girl."

"Yeah, I think you do," Frankie agreed.

Fletch's head tilted as he studied him. "I don't know that I've ever told you this, but you're a damn good man, Frankie. I was sure when Annie told us she was gonna marry you someday, that she'd grow out of it. I couldn't deal with her even *thinking* about that when she was seven. But as Emily and I got to know you over the years, and saw how devoted you are to her, we realized that you were literally perfect for each other. I appreciate the sacrifices you've made to support her—"

"I haven't made any sacrifices," Frankie interrupted. "Not one. I'd move to a new city every damn year of my life if it meant being with her. No job is more important than Annie. Nothing is."

"See? That's what I'm talking about," Fletch said. "All I

ever want for my kids is for them to find someone who loves them as much as I love my Emily. And the two of you have a connection that can't be explained. It's as if you were meant for each other from the moment you were conceived. I can't explain it any other way."

Frankie liked that. No, he *loved* that.

"Anyway, I consider you one of my sons, Frankie. Even if you and Annie never get married, you'll always be a part of my family. I hope if you ever need anything, you won't hesitate to come to me. I know your dad feels the same way, as does Cooper...so I just want you to know I'm right there with them."

"Thank you," Frankie said quietly. He'd always been a bit intimidated by Annie's dad and her unofficial uncles. They were larger than life. Strong. Badass. He was nothing like them, except in one way. The most important.

He'd do whatever it took to keep Annie safe.

His lack of hearing didn't make him less smart than anyone else. It didn't make him less capable. But to many others, it made him weak or weird. Somehow less of a man.

Annie had been the first person in his life, other than his dad, to treat him as if he was whole. His lack of hearing hadn't turned her off or made things awkward between them. Her enthusiasm and complete acceptance were among the many qualities that made him fall in love with her so quickly. Even at seven years old, Frankie knew a good thing when he saw it. And he was smart enough to know he wanted to keep her forever.

"Any chance I can get you to head to the kitchen and

kick my daughter out so I can have a chat with her?"
Fletch asked.

"Of course," Frankie said. "I know I don't have to say
this, but I'm going to anyway. Go easy. This could be the
most important talk you have with your daughter in her
life."

Instead of blowing him off, Fletch nodded. "That bad?"

"It's not bad," Frankie said. "She just loves and admires
you so much, you have the power to crush her if she
doesn't have your support."

Fletch sighed. "I'd rather cut off my arm than do
anything to hurt my little girl."

"She's not ten anymore," Frankie warned him.

"I know. Believe me, I know. You sure you can't give me
a hint?" Fletch asked hopefully.

"I've probably already said too much," Frankie said.
"For the record? I told her she had nothing to worry about
and that you wouldn't be disappointed in her. Please don't
make a liar out of me. I'd hate to have to spend my vacation picking up the pieces of her broken heart."

Fletch nodded, and Frankie stood. "I'll go get her."

"Frankie?"

He turned at the office door and looked at Fletch.
"Yeah?"

"She's got me wrapped around her little finger. I won't
let her down. Or you."

Frankie lifted his chin and Fletch returned the gesture.
As he headed for the kitchen, he couldn't help but
remember once upon a time when Cooper had taught him
that chin lift. He'd said it was a secret greeting for men.

He'd felt so grown-up and mature, and over the last twenty years, the gesture had become second nature.

It still surprised him sometimes that he'd been so readily accepted by Cooper and his SEAL friends. Or that he got along so well with Annie's father and his Delta teammates. He wasn't anything like them, and yet they'd welcomed him into the fold without blinking. Frankie knew a large part of that was because of Annie, but it still felt good. As if maybe he wasn't as nerdy or as much of an oddball as he'd always felt around other people.

He headed for the kitchen, and Annie turned to look at him as he approached. "Hey, your dad was hoping he could have a few words with you," Frankie told her.

A panicked look crossed Annie's face for a moment, before she quickly hid it.

Frankie couldn't stay away if he tried. He walked up to her, took the measuring spoon and bottle of vanilla extract out of her hand, and pulled her out of the room. "I'll be right back, Mrs. Fletcher. I can help with the cookies."

"No rush, Frankie!" Emily said with a smile. "Take your time."

Frankie pulled Annie into the hallway that led to her dad's office. Then he stopped and took her face in his hands. "Breathe, love," he ordered.

Annie grabbed hold of his wrists. "What did you tell him?" she asked nervously.

"Nothing."

She frowned. "Why not?"

Frankie blinked. "Because I'd never break your confidence."

"It would've been easier if you had," she sighed.

He frowned. Shit. Should he have warned Fletch after all?

No. He trusted Annie's dad, even if *she* didn't right now. She was understandably nervous, but he had no doubt that Fletch would do the right thing by his daughter. He'd support her unconditionally.

Frankie leaned forward and kissed Annie's forehead. Then he pulled her into him and held her close. He was only a few inches taller, and she fit against him perfectly. After hugging her gently, ever aware that while her ribs had almost completely healed, they still hurt if she moved too fast, Frankie set her back from him. He put his hands on her shoulders. "This is your dad," he reminded her. "He loves you. It'll be fine. Just tell him what you told me. He'll understand."

"I hope so," she fretted.

"He will," Frankie said confidently. "Now, how much damage control do I need to do in the kitchen?"

Annie rolled her eyes and smacked his shoulder, as he'd expected her to. "I did exactly what my mom told me to. I wasn't going to risk messing up her precious cookies."

"Smart." His Annie could kick military ass, but she couldn't cook worth a damn. That was fine; Frankie could. It was just another way they complemented each other perfectly.

He stood back and spoke using sign language. *It's a good thing your dad put us out in the guesthouse. I'm not sure he would approve of the things I want to do to his daughter under his own roof.*

Annie giggled, as Frankie had hoped. She signed back,

I think he should be more worried about the things I want to do to you.

Frankie shook his head. Damn, he loved this woman. *Go. Talk to your dad. You'll both feel better. If I'm not in the kitchen when you're done, I'll be waiting for you in our room. I love you.*

Love you too, Annie signed. Then she stepped into him, kissed him hard, and turned to head to her dad's office. Her shoulders straight and her chin up.

Frankie wanted to tell her that she didn't need to put up her shields to talk to her dad, but he figured she'd realize that soon enough. While he worried about how the conversation would go, Frankie had no doubt that Fletch would handle his daughter exactly right. He loved her and wanted the best for her. There was no way Annie could disappoint him. No way in hell.

CHAPTER SIX

Annie shoved her emotions down deep inside. It was what she did when she went into battle, and while this wasn't exactly the same, she couldn't help but want to protect herself. On the one hand, she didn't think her dad would be upset with her for maybe wanting to get out of the Army, but a small part of her wasn't one hundred percent sure.

Cormac Fletcher was a career military man from the top of his head to the tips of his toes. He lived and breathed the Army and was both respected and revered in Delta Force circles. All of his teammates were. They'd earned their reputations.

But to Annie, he was her Daddy Fletch. He was the man who'd literally saved her and her mom's lives. He'd been the guy who'd told her she could be anyone she wanted to be, do anything she wanted to do. Had encouraged her and pushed her to be the best soldier and officer she could be.

The very last thing she wanted to do was let him down.

To make him feel as if she didn't appreciate everything he'd done for her. If it hadn't been for his encouragement, she never would've gotten to where she was today. And now she was going to tell him there was a possibility she wanted to get out of the Army. That she wasn't sure it was what she wanted anymore.

God. She couldn't do this.

The office door opened just as Annie was about to flee down the hall. Her dad always seemed to have a sixth sense for knowing where she was. The one time she'd tried to sneak out of the house in high school, he'd caught her even though she knew she hadn't made one damn sound. It was almost uncanny, but that was her dad.

"Hi," she squeaked.

"Hey, sprite. I didn't hear any explosions, so you must not have blown up the kitchen," Fletch teased.

"Whatever, Dad," she said with a roll of her eyes.

Reaching out, Fletch took her hand and tugged her gently into the office, closing the door behind them. He led her over to the leather sofa and, once she was seated, parked himself right beside her. He still held her hand, and it comforted Annie. Fletch had always seemed to be able to do that for her. Just his presence made her problems disappear.

"It's good to see you. It's been too long since you've been home," Fletch said.

"I know. Things have been crazy at work. One mission after another."

"I'm glad you were able to get your leave time approved."

"Me too. But it was pretty easy since the team is short-handed right now. It'll take time for the Army to get new guys in, for them to be brought up to speed. I'll be busy when I get back, training them and teaching them how our team operates, but for now, I'm going to enjoy the downtime."

"Tex sent me the video of your jump into that chopper. Pretty impressive, sprite."

Annie winced. Having a guy with connections on top of connections was useful, but at times, it was also a pain in the ass. Most soldiers today wore body cams, to protect themselves against claims of brutality, as well as to protect the civilians from excessive force by the military who entered their country. She hadn't thought much about it, but wasn't surprised the men in the helicopter had caught her death-defying leap on camera. Or that Tex had somehow gotten ahold of the footage and shared it with her dad.

"Your ribs feel okay?" he asked when she didn't immediately say anything.

"They're good," she said.

"You want to talk about it?" Fletch asked. "That situation looked pretty intense."

"Not really. It never should've happened. We were ambushed, and by the grace of God, we all made it out alive," Annie said succinctly, summing up the horrific hours she and her team had been pinned down by enemy fire. She didn't want to talk about how she'd thought for a while that she'd never see Frankie or her family again. "Can I ask you something, Dad?"

"You can ask me anything," Fletch confirmed.

Annie resisted the urge to roll her eyes again. She knew

she could *ask* anything, but it was a crapshoot whether or not he'd actually answer. Throughout the years, she'd tried to get details about his missions, but he'd stayed true to his vow to the Army and his Delta team, keeping what they did a secret from everyone, including his family. "How'd you get to stay here in Texas for so long? I mean, the Army isn't known for letting its soldiers stay at one base for much longer than two or three years. You and your team were here for years before you retired."

Fletch nodded. "Yeah, we were lucky. We made a deal with the Army."

"A deal?" Annie asked.

"Yeah. We said we'd stay in for twenty-five years if we got to keep Fort Hood as our duty station."

"Seriously? That's it?"

Her dad looked uncomfortable for a moment. "Well, not exactly."

"Let me guess, Tex helped," Annie said with a laugh.

Fletch smiled. "Yeah, he did. But to be fair, there was a shortage of teams at that time. The Army was desperate to keep Deltas from leaving. We got lucky, and we know it."

Annie nodded and looked down at her fingers, intertwined in her lap.

"You've been moved quite a few times," Fletch said. "How does Frankie feel about that?"

"You know him. He doesn't complain. But it's gotten old for me," Annie admitted. Knowing it was now or never, she plunged ahead. "When I joined the Army, I thought I'd be a lifer, like you. I thought I'd bond with my team like you did with yours, and we'd be this tight, cohesive unit. But I've had so many men funneled in and out of my team, I can't even remember all their names. They're all pretty young too, and I haven't found that I have much in common with them at all. I've liked all of them, but my rank as an officer has kept us from getting close as well... fraternization and all that."

"The bond I have with Ghost, Hollywood, and the others is special. Unique," Fletch said.

"I know. But I still had hopes that I'd find that too. But instead, Frankie and I sit at home between missions by ourselves. Don't get me wrong, I love being with Frankie, and there's no one I'd rather hang out with, but I guess I just envisioned going out to bars or spending time at my teammates' houses...like you guys did when I was growing up."

She paused.

Fletch covered her hands with one of his large ones. "What else?"

Annie looked up at him. "What else *what*?"

"What else is on your mind? It's obvious you've got a lot weighing on you. Get it all out. You've always been able to talk to me in the past, nothing's changed. I've got your back, sprite."

He did. Annie knew that. But she hadn't even gotten to the hard part yet. "I want to marry Frankie. He's all I've ever wanted. But something always seems to come up. I know Mom wants a huge wedding, like she had, and just when I think I'm ready to talk to her about it, I get deployed."

"Maybe you're putting it off because you aren't sure it's what you *truly* want," Fletch suggested.

"No!" Annie exclaimed heatedly. "I love Frankie, Dad.

He's literally the best thing to ever happen to me...but I can't help but think he deserves *better*. He's so smart, and he could be using his engineering degree in some kick-ass company somewhere, but instead he's following me around the country making a third of what he could be as a counselor for the VA. I'm holding him back, and I can't help but feel as if I'm gonna come home from a deployment someday to him telling me he's done. That he can't take the Army lifestyle anymore."

"That boy's loved you just as long as you've loved him," Fletch reprimanded gently. "I see the same thing in his eyes when he looks at you that I feel when I look at your mom. He's not going anywhere. And I'm almost one hundred percent positive that he doesn't care about what he does for a living, as long as he gets to be with you. You both had a very hard time making it through your college careers without being together. I'm proud of you both. Not many relationships can withstand the test of time that yours has."

"Thanks, Dad," Annie said.

"I have a feeling that's not what's really bothering you," Fletch said.

This was it. It was time. "It's not," Annie agreed. She took a deep breath and looked up at her dad. "I'm considering getting out of the Army."

Not one emotion crossed Fletch's face. "Why?"

Annie sighed. "It's a lot of things. Definitely because of the things I've already talked about. But I kind of had an epiphany on the side of that mountain, Dad. Regret. Anger at the Army for taking me away from Frankie so much. I started to wonder if all my sacrifices were worth it. And I *hate* that I felt that way. Still feel that way. All I've ever wanted to do was be in the military. In the Special Forces. I can't stand the thought of letting everyone down. Of letting *you* down."

"Oh, sprite. You've never let me down in your entire life. Not once. I don't care if you quit and decide to become a street artist, making a living by panhandling for tips. I'm proud of you no matter what you do."

Annie couldn't stop the tears from falling. "I saw your face every time I got promoted. When I graduated from Green Beret training and made the teams. And when I was put in charge of my own unit. You can't deny that."

"I can't, and I won't. I *am* proud of all that you've accomplished. You're an amazing woman, an amazing soldier. But that doesn't mean I won't be proud of you if you quit and do something else. Part of being a parent is supporting your kids no matter what they do in life. I might not always understand or agree with your decisions, but they aren't *my* decisions to make."

"So you don't agree with me wanting to quit?" Annie asked, her stomach clenching in distress.

"I didn't say that. Look at me, sprite."

Annie did as her dad requested, meeting his gaze head on.

"You are not me. I am not you. You have to make your own way in the world. I know if you leave the Army, it's *their* loss. You're a hell of an officer. You care about your team in a way not a lot of soldiers do. You've given one hundred percent of your time and effort in the last six years to being the best Green Beret you can be. But I'd *never* want you to continue doing something if your heart isn't in it. That's a surefire way to get injured or killed, especially in your profession. You're twenty-seven, sprite, not seven—as much as I hate to admit it, because that makes me even older—and your mom and I have raised you to be smart and independent. To be able to make your own decisions. If you want to know the truth, part of me is thrilled you're considering getting out."

Annie gaped at him. "Seriously?"

"Of course. You forget I know exactly what you're doing. I have a perspective most people don't. I saw that video Tex sent me, and while I didn't see the preceding hours before you made that leap into that helicopter, I can imagine the hell you went through. As your dad, I'm relieved you won't be in that position in the future. I don't like it when people shoot at my little girl. Try to kill my sprite."

Annie was so relieved, she closed her eyes.

"But...you have to be sure of your decision."

Annie opened her eyes and looked at her dad.

"Once you decide to get out, that's it. There's no going back. There are a lot of perks to being in the Army. Health insurance, housing, life insurance, job security, the retirement...to name a few. Regret is a hard thing to deal with. The last thing I want is you deciding you want out, only to regret your decision later. You can't go back once you quit, Annie. So you have to be one hundred percent sure before you make that call."

He was right, Annie knew he was, but it was still hard to hear. "Did you ever have second thoughts?"

"Yes."

Annie couldn't help but be surprised yet again. Fletch

was one of those men who was born to be a soldier. He lived and breathed it.

"It's not an easy life," he told her. "You know that as well as I do. But I loved being a Delta. There was no job I could think of outside of the Army that would fulfill me as much as being a soldier did. Did I love everything about it? No, of course not. But I was willing to put up with the things I disliked in order to keep doing what I loved. What I was made to do." He took a breath. "As long as I've known you, you've been drawn to military life. From those obstacle courses you ran, to the plastic Army men you threw out of your flower basket at my and your mom's wedding. Crawling in the dirt was always more appealing than dressing up. You've worked your ass off to get where you are, so I just want you to consider all angles and be sure, sprite."

Annie nodded, feeling a little sick inside. Her dad was giving her good advice, but it still seemed as if she was letting him down for even thinking about leaving the Army...which sucked. She knew that had less to do with his words than with her own confusion and uncertainty. Which wasn't something her dad could fix.

He held out his arm. "Come 'ere," he ordered gently.

Annie snuggled into her father, not caring that she wasn't seven anymore. She loved and respected this man with everything she had. He'd been the one to *teach* her what love was. How a man should treat a woman. He'd set the bar extremely high, but Frankie had more than met it.

"What do you think you want to do...if you get out, that is?" Fletch asked as he stroked her hair, holding her close.

"I'm thinking maybe med school."

Fletch snorted in amusement. "Only you would be worried I'd be disappointed you were quitting the Army to become a doctor."

Annie lifted her head. "Except you love the Army."

"So do you. That doesn't mean you have to make it your career just because I did. What specialty are you thinking?"

"I think trauma. There's something extremely fulfilling about being able to help someone who's sustained a critical injury, or even on the verge of death, and bring them back. Make them whole again. I know more than most that it doesn't always end up well, but I like the challenge. Besides, can you see me being a pediatrician? Or a podiatrist?"

Her dad chuckled. "No. If you go that route, you're gonna be an asset to any emergency room you end up in," he said with no hint of doubt.

Annie eyed her dad. "Are you sure Frankie didn't give you a head's up as to what I wanted to talk about?"

"Definitely. I *wanted* him to. Gave him every opportunity to spill the beans. But that man is completely loyal to you, sprite."

Annie's heart seemed to grow in size. He *was* completely loyal. She knew that. Frankie wouldn't break a confidence or betray her. No way.

"Med school isn't going to be easy," Annie muttered.

"And becoming a Green Beret was?" Fletch asked with a lift of an eyebrow.

It was Annie's turn to laugh. "No, but there are gonna be long nights and I'm going to have to study a lot. I'm just not sure that's fair to Frankie. He's stood by me with the Army thing, and I hate to do this to him too."

"Do what to him?" Fletch asked. "The way I see it, he'll be thrilled. You'll be home a hell of a lot more than you are now, and as a bonus, it's a lot safer. If it bothers you enough, why don't you ask him where he wants to work? If he could be hired anywhere, if he could have any job in the world, what would he want that to be and where? Then find a med school near his dream location."

Annie nodded and wiped her cheeks free of the tears she'd shed earlier. "That's a great idea."

"I know," Fletch said smugly. "And just sayin', there are some great engineering jobs here in Texas, as well as VA hospitals. And the University of Texas, A&M, Baylor, Texas Tech...they're all here too and have great med schools."

Annie shook her head at her dad. "I thought you said to ask Frankie where *he* wanted to work."

"I did. But that doesn't mean you can't nudge him. I'd love to have you closer, sprite. Your mom and I have missed you. As have your brothers."

"So you think I should do it? Quit the Army and go to med school?"

"I can't make this decision for you, Annie."

"Darn it," she muttered.

Fletch chuckled. "I can't deny having you closer would be amazing, but having you follow in my footsteps is also a dream come true for me. You have to make your decision based on what *you* want, sprite. Not me. Or your mom. Or anyone else...except maybe Frankie."

Annie hated this. She'd kinda hoped talking to

Fletch would help her make this decision. He'd either tell her she was crazy for thinking about quitting the Army, or he'd tell her in no uncertain terms that getting out was the right decision. Instead, he'd brought up good points for both staying and leaving. And even though she heard him when he'd said she had to make the decision for herself, the fact remained that if she quit...it would feel as if she was turning her back on the profession her dad loved down to the very marrow of his bones.

"I've missed all of you guys too," Annie said after a long pause. "Dad?"

"Yeah?"

"Thanks for being such a great role model. When you and Mom got married, you didn't even hesitate to step into the role of my dad, and I couldn't have asked for a better man to show me what it meant to be loved."

"You're very loved," Fletch said, his voice catching. "I'm so damn proud of you, Ann Elizabeth Grant Fletcher."

She laughed. "The only people who call me Ann, let alone use my middle name, is Mom when she's upset with me and people at work."

"Yeah, you'll always be Annie to me. But seriously, you were such a smart, inquisitive kid, I knew you were going to either be the world's best criminal, or you'd do noble things with that mind of yours."

Annie laughed again.

"And, you didn't let my bozo friends spoil you *too* rotten," Fletch said. "I swear, every time I turned around someone was building you a tank, or taking you to the post to run through the obstacle course, or buying you some military toy or uniform."

Annie smiled, remembering how great her childhood had been. "Are all the guys going to be here tomorrow?"

"If by 'all the guys' you mean Ghost, Coach, Hollywood, Beatle, Blade, Truck, Trigger, Lefty, Brain, Oz, Lucky, Doc, and Grover...yes."

Annie beamed. "All of them? And their wives too?"

"Yup. And a lot of the kids, from what I hear. You know no one can resist a party," Fletch said.

"Man, I haven't seen the cousins in so long," Annie said wistfully. Her dad's friends' children weren't really cousins, but because everyone was so close, they might as well have been.

"Well, you'll see them tomorrow. Everyone is growing up so fast. Gillian and Trigger's twins are five already."

"Holy cow, wasn't it just last year they had them?" Annie asked.

Her dad laughed. "It seems like it. And Casey and Beatle's little girl is nine."

"Please tell me she likes bugs like her mom does," Annie said.

"Oh yeah, much to Beatle's consternation," Fletch replied.

Annie's smile faded. "Thanks for not freaking out on me. I know I kind of sprung the whole getting-out-of-the-Army thing on you."

"It's your life, sprite, not mine. I hate that you had even a moment of worry about how I'd react though."

"It's just that I admire you so much, and the absolute last thing I ever want is to disappoint you."

"I've been watching videos of your missions for years," Fletch said, surprising Annie. "And every last one scared the shit out of me. You've had some very close calls, and somehow you've always managed to get yourself and your team out alive. You're damn good at what you do. No matter what derogatory things some people might say about females being in the Green Berets, you've proven them wrong. You're at the top of your game. Period."

"Dad..." Annie whispered, feeling even more like he was urging her to stick it out.

"You have nothing to be ashamed of for thinking about leaving. You've served your country with grace and dignity, and you've more than earned the accolades you have in that shoebox under your bed. Whatever decision you make, make it with your head up, sprite. You're a hell of an officer, a hell of a Green Beret, and a hell of a soldier. Always will be, no matter if you get out now or in another fifteen years."

Closing her eyes, feeling no closer to a decision than when she'd entered her dad's office, Annie sighed as he hugged her a bit tighter, kissing the top of her head. "I kind of wanted you to tell me I was insane for even thinking about getting out, or to quit and never look back."

Fletch snorted. "I can't make this decision for you."

"I wish you would."

"You'll do the right thing for *you*," her dad told her without any sign of misgiving in his tone.

"I'm scared, Dad," she admitted. "All my life, I've wanted to be in the military. I'm not sure I even know how to do anything else. What if I quit and fail out of med school?"

"What was that thing your mom used to say to you about being brave?" Fletch asked.

"Being scared means you're about to do something really brave," Annie recited.

"Yeah, that's the one. It's no wonder you're apprehensive about what the future holds. You've done what the Army's told you to do, gone where they've told you to go, and all you've been able to concentrate on is staying alive long enough to head out on the next mission. You've got your entire life ahead of you. You and Frankie. Thinking hard about what you want and making a decision about your future is damn courageous of you."

Annie wasn't sure about that. She didn't feel courageous. She felt confused and almost sick inside. But she didn't let any of that show through when she said, "I love you, Dad."

"I love you too. Now...you hungry for a cookie?"

Annie laughed. "You gonna risk Mom's wrath by stealing one?" she asked.

"Yup. But we can be a team. You and Frankie distract her and I'll move in for the kill."

God, Annie loved her dad. He was a goof. "Sounds like a plan," she agreed.

Fletch stood and pulled her up with him. He put a hand on her cheek. "You good, sprite?"

"I'm good," Annie confirmed. Or she was as good as she was going to get at that moment. She didn't know what her decision would be about the military, but she felt better knowing her dad would support her regardless.

Before they walked out of the office, Annie asked, "You think Mom's ready to help me plan a wedding?"

Fletch beamed. "Just say the word. She'll pull out the huge binder she's been stuffing pamphlets and other wedding crap into for years."

Annie giggled. "Do you think we could have the reception here?"

Fletch stopped and stared down at her. "Really?"

"Well, yeah. I've got so many awesome memories here. The yard is huge and will more than fit everyone. And I know you've got the best security system, so there won't be another surprise robbery like the one that happened at *your* reception."

Fletch winced. "I'm never going to live that down," he mumbled.

"And can I request that no one use an RPG and burn down the house at our reception too, please?" Annie asked with a grin.

"Hey, *that* wasn't my fault," Fletch protested.

Annie hooked her arm with her dad's as they headed for the door. "I know," she soothed. "And I have to admit that I liked my room better here anyway. It was bigger."

"You just love that huge walk-in closet I added for you."

She did, but Annie would never admit it. "Tell me you've still got that tank around here somewhere. I bet everyone would love to play with it tomorrow."

"Of course I do. You think I'd throw that thing away?" Fletch asked. "Maybe I can get the guys to help me put in a remote control and we can bring your rings down the aisle in it."

Annie rolled her eyes. "No, Dad. Leave the wedding planning to Mom."

"Spoilsport," Fletch complained.

They entered the living room and made a beeline for the kitchen. Annie saw her mom's gaze go straight to her husband's, as if she was making sure everything was all right. She was okay with coming in second with her mom, because Annie's eyes were glued to Frankie. He'd donned an apron, and the moment he saw her, he put down the spoon he was using to ladle dough onto a cookie pan and came toward her.

Everything okay? he signed.

Yeah, Annie signed back. Then she was in his arms. Every time he hugged her, Annie felt as if she was coming home. It had always been that way with him. No matter how much time had passed since they saw each other. One month, one week, one year. She always felt better when his arms closed around her. She might be a badass soldier, but this was what kept her going. Knowing Frankie loved her.

CHAPTER SEVEN

"Annie!"

It felt like the millionth time she'd heard her name called, but Annie turned with a smile anyway. She loved this. Loved being surrounded by the people she adored and had grown up with. This time, it was Truck who'd called her name.

Beaming as one of her favorite people on the planet picked her up and swung her in a circle, Annie looked up when he put her back on her feet. Truck was huge. At six foot seven, he towered over most people, her included. Not only that, but he was extremely muscular. Even though he wasn't active duty anymore, he obviously hadn't stopped working out.

She lifted a hand to Truck's cheek, covering the gnarly scar on one side of his face. "Hey, Truck," she said happily.

"It's been too long since you've been home," he complained.

Annie smiled at that. Truck had always been a bit

grumpier than her dad's other friends, but she loved him all the same. "It hasn't been that long," she countered.

"Long enough," Truck told her. "Your man here?"

"Of course. Last I saw him, he was with some of the kids, teaching thcm naughty things to say via sign language," Annie said.

Truck laughed. "That sounds like something Frankie would do."

"How're Ford and Elizabeth? I haven't seen them yet."

"They're not here. Ford's off at college taking summer courses, and Elizabeth is on a date."

Annie couldn't help but laugh at the look of disgust on Truck's face. "She's what, sixteen or seventeen?"

"Seventeen."

"Which is plenty old enough to date, Truck," Annie admonished.

"Nope. I was hoping she wouldn't be interested in that kind of thing until she was twenty-five or six."

Annie rolled her eyes at the big teddy bear. "You know that's ridiculous," she scolded.

"It's not. But it's okay. I made sure her date knew if he did anything out of line, he'd answer to mc," Truck said with a small smirk.

"What'd you do?" Annie asked, already grinning.

"He decided to clean his guns when the young man arrived to pick up Elizabeth," a woman about Annie's height said as she came up beside Truck.

"Mary!" Annie exclaimed in delight, hugging Truck's wife.

"How are you?" Mary asked.

"I'm good. You look great. Love the green hair."

"Thanks. I decided to try something new."

"It fits you."

And it did. Mary was one of a kind. She was blunt and outspoken, and Annie loved her all the more for it. She could always count on Truck's wife to tell her the truth when she needed to hear it.

"I heard you're thinking about getting out of the Army," Mary said.

Annie wrinkled her nose. It never failed to amaze her how fast her dad's friends spread gossip. But in this case, it actually worked in her favor. She hadn't had to make any big announcements about her future plans. She might've been upset with Fletch for spreading the news so quickly, but he'd done her a favor. And he was probably well aware that it would prevent her from having the same difficult conversation over and over.

"Yup," Annie said simply.

"Good for you," Mary said. "I was the first one to think you breaking into the ranks of the Green Berets was awesome, but if it doesn't make you happy anymore, fuck it. Life's too short to stay in a job you aren't passionate about...more so if said job can literally kill you."

Annie smiled. "Thanks." It was obvious Mary was one hundred percent supportive of her getting out of the Army, acting as if the decision had already been made. Truck's wife was never afraid to share her opinion, which was one of a million reasons why Annie adored her.

"I bet Frankie is thrilled," Truck said as he wrapped his arm around Mary and pulled her close.

"We haven't talked specifics about what happens if I *do*

make that decision," Annie admitted. "But I don't think he's gonna protest me not being shot at if I decide to get out."

"Can we not talk about you being shot?" Truck grumbled.

Annie and Mary both laughed.

"Come on, girl, let's go chat about this cruise you have coming up. It sounds amazeballs," Mary said. She went up on tiptoes to kiss Truck, then wrapped her arm around Annie's and pulled her away.

Annie waved at Truck, who gave her one of those manly chin lifts her dad's friends were wont to do, and allowed Mary to lead her outside to a group of women. When Annie's mom had said she'd invited everyone, she hadn't lied.

The yard was completely full of people. There were a ton of teenagers—Doug's friends who had also just graduated, as well as Annie's cousins. Her dad was in charge of the four grills that were currently smoking, making hamburgers and hotdogs nonstop for all the hungry mouths at the party.

Not only were all of her dad's former teammates and their families present, the other Delta team her dad had gotten to know over the years was there as well. Annie saw Chase and Sadie's sixteen-year-old son flirting with Oz and Riley's niece, Bria. Her brother John was hanging out with Kinley and Lefty's son, Dominic, and Aspen and Brain's son, Chance, were over in a quiet corner. Who knew what the threesome was talking about. Probably plotting to take over the world.

Frankie was sitting at a table with Riley and Oz's

daughters, Amalia and Brittney, and Ember and Doc's daughter, Jemila. Annie thought they were all in their early teens, and all three girls looked at Frankie as if enthralled. Because he was also signing as he spoke, Annie could see he was telling the girls about some of the people he worked with at the VA hospital.

"He's a good man," Mary said quietly from next to her.

Annie turned to smile at the other woman. "He is," she agreed.

"Come on, I know the girls want to hear all about your upcoming cruise."

Annie let herself be led over to where a large group of women was sitting. She'd already said hello to most of them. Rayne, Harley, Kassie, Casey, Wendy, Gillian, Kinley, Aspen, Riley, Ember, and Sierra were all there. Annie still had a hard time wrapping her mind around the fact that *the* Ember Maxwell—now Wagner—was someone she called a friend. In the twelve or so years since she'd met the ex-Olympian and famous social media star, she'd only become more well-known. But now it was for her passionate and tireless work for people who'd gone missing, and for her philanthropic work for the less fortunate.

"Hey," Annie said as she sat in the one empty chair amongst the women. "Is this the hot seat or what?" she quipped.

"If the shoe fits," Rayne said with a grin.

"How're you feeling? Hollywood told me about your broken ribs," Kassie said.

"And I didn't see the video, but I heard all about that wild leap you made into that helicopter," Gillian said with a grimace.

"Piece of cake for our Special Forces sensation," Aspen said with a wink in Annie's direction.

"I'm good, thanks," Annie said, answering Rayne's question. "Mostly all healed, I just get a twinge every now and then. I still can't get over the fact that some of you—and probably *all* the guys—have seen that video, when I haven't. It's not like it's on the 'net or anything. Jeez."

"You know how our guys are," Casey said with a shrug.

"Yeah, they think that stuff is cool and are overeager to share," Kinley agreed.

"And we only recognize you because we know you," Wendy added.

"Right. And we have no idea where the video was taken," Sierra said.

Annie simply shook her head. She wasn't really upset that all the guys had shared the video with their wives. It *was* a hell of a jump, she could admit that.

"Anyway, enough about that. You're probably sick of talking about getting out of the Army—which, by the way, I completely support," Rayne said.

"The thought of someone trying to kill you mission after mission makes my skin crawl," Harley said.

"Right? Like, who the hell would want to kill our little Annie?" Kassie asked rhetorically.

"Idiots, that's who," Harley said. "And I'm totally using that jump in my next *This is War* game. I'm gonna make it hella hard to successfully get in that chopper. You only made it look easy because of all the time you spent on those obstacle courses."

"I remember watching you for the first time when you were around twelve or thirteen," Gillian said. "I knew you were gonna grow up to be someone amazing when I saw you help another kid get through the course. You didn't care about winning, you just wanted that boy to feel good about making it through himself."

"All right, enough," Annie said with a small chuckle. "I'm amazing and awesome, blah blah blah, can we change the subject?" She knew she was blushing, and she needed everyone to talk about something else. She loved their support, and felt blessed to be surrounded by so many kind people, but sometimes she struggled to live up to the praise.

"But wait, you haven't already decided you're getting out, right?" Aspen asked.

Annie shrugged. "No."

"Good," Aspen said.

"You think she should stay in?" Rayne asked.

"Well, yeah. She's worked her ass off to get where she is. She's finally showing all the men who said a woman could never succeed in Special Forces where they can shove that nonsense."

"But *you* got out," Harley pointed out, not unkindly.

"I did, but this is *Annie* we're talking about," Aspen said. "She was born to be a soldier."

"That's true," Wendy agreed.

"I remember hearing the story about when you were ten and threw a huge conniption fit about having to wear a dress to some ball or something on post," Gillian said with a smile. "You got your way and were able to wear camo pants and an Amy-green shirt. You were the belle of the ball anyway, with all the soldiers saluting you all night."

Everyone chuckled and continued to reminisce, telling

stories about Annie's Army dreams since childhood. How proud all their husbands were when she'd graduated from basic training.

The more they talked, the more nauseous Annie felt.

Previously, she'd only been worried about letting her dad and the guys down if she quit. Now it seemed she'd be disappointing their wives, as well.

Eventually, the other women noticed that Annie wasn't participating in their conversation.

"Sorry, didn't mean to go on and on," Aspen said with a smile. "But seriously, I can't imagine you doing anything but being in the Army."

"Same," Gillian said.

"But we'd get to see her more if she did something else," Rayne insisted.

"Not to mention it'd be safer," Harley said.

Mary held up her hands. "Right. How about we stop freaking Annie out," she said sternly.

Annie shot her a small grateful smile. She couldn't deny she *was* a little freaked out.

"Annie's gonna do what she's gonna do, and we'll all support her no matter what. Can we change the subject and talk about how much sex she's gonna have on her cruise?" Mary said, completely straight-faced.

"Oh, Lord, let's not," Rayne said with a groan. "I still picture Annie as she was when I met her."

"But seriously...Frankie grew into a fine-looking young man," Kassie said.

Annie looked over at Frankie again and couldn't agree more with her mom's friend.

"He reminds me of Brain," Aspen said with a smile. "At

first glance, people underestimate my husband because they think he's nothing more than a nerd who can speak a million languages. But when provoked, he turns into a grizzly bear, ready to defend his family and friends no matter what it takes."

Annie had to agree with Aspen's assessment. Frankie had worked very hard his entire life to be seen as equal to his peers. He'd been just as smart, or more so, than others in his classes. But because of his obvious disability, he'd been passed over time and time again for opportunities he would've kicked ass at. He also never hesitated to protect her when they were out and about, and someone got a bit too mouthy or felt the need to be an asshole. She was a deadly Special Forces soldier, yet her fiancé didn't care. She was his to protect. Period.

It used to bother her. She didn't want Frankie to get hurt in an altercation because of her, and she hated when people found out about his disability and tried to belittle him. But after a talk with Fletch, she understood that she should be thanking her lucky stars she had a partner who loved her enough to physically put himself between her and whatever he deemed a threat.

"He's pretty amazing," Annie said after a beat.

"Tell us more about this cruise you're going on," Sierra said. "How many people are on this boat?"

"Ship. And I think around sixty or so? I'm not really sure," Annie said.

"And it's a sailboat?" Casey asked.

"Yes. But a really big one," Annie said with a laugh. "It's got four pole thingies with the sails on them."

"You mean masts?" Rayne asked.

"I guess. Is that what they're called?" Annie asked.

"Lord, woman," Mary said with a shake of her head. "It's a good thing you're in the Army. The Navy would've kicked you out for calling a mast a 'pole thingy.'"

Everyone laughed.

"Anyway, I guess the ship is fairly old. Some rich people owned it in the twenties, and it's changed ownership several times over the years. Additional rooms were added, and a cruise company bought it. Because it's so small—for a cruise kind of ship, that is—it can go to islands in the Caribbean that the bigger ships can't," Annie explained.

"Like where?" Ember asked.

"No clue," Annie admitted. "Honestly, I've never heard of most of them. Frankie is super stoked though. He looked them all up and has been studying the history of each of the islands. I'm sure my eyes will glaze over when he starts spitting out all the info he learned."

Everyone chuckled.

"I guess the cruise line owns some huge private island that we'll be stopping at too. Well...they don't own the whole thing, but a section of it. The beach part. The north side is rocky all the way to the ocean, and the south side is a picture-perfect beach with lots of trees and a long strip of sand. The pictures online of the area the cruise line owns looked beautiful," Annie explained, getting excited about the upcoming trip all over again.

"But you don't like swimming," Rayne said in confusion.

"True, but I like being by the ocean," Annie explained.

"I like walking in the sand, wading in the water, and having the sea breeze in my face."

"Another reason the Navy would've kicked you out by now," Mary quipped.

"How'd you find out about this ship?" Gillian asked.

"How do you think?" Annie asked with a laugh. "Tex sent me a brochure."

Once again, the entire group burst out laughing.

"Is he making you take a tracker?" Harley asked.

"No. But I'm sure he'll be keeping his eye on the ship the entire trip," Annie said. The truth was, she adored Tex, so if he told her he'd feel more comfortable with her taking one of his infamous trackers, she'd do it, no questions asked. She'd seen firsthand how important they would be and how many lives had been saved by the devices. But he'd done his research on the cruise company and the ship they'd be on, and no red flags had come up. If they had, Annie knew he never would've recommended the trip.

She sat with the women for another forty-five minutes, enjoying the various conversations, ranging from Riley and Oz's son, Logan's success on his minor league baseball team, to Gillian's twins' latest mishap of seeing how far they could stick various objects up their noses.

Over the years, Annie had become less of "one of the kids" and more of a friend. And she couldn't be happier about that. For a while, she'd thought she'd forever be seven in their eyes, but gradually they'd come to the real-ization that she'd grown into an independent woman.

At one point, she looked over to where Frankie had been sitting with the girls and saw he was now alone, staring at her. She asked him via sign if everything was all right, and he signed back that he was fine, he was just sitting there wondering how in the world he'd gotten so lucky.

Annie blushed, looking forward to their vacation more and more as it got closer. She adored her family and friends, but she craved alone time with her fiancé.

"I know that look," Aspen whispered from next to Annie.

"What look?" she asked, tearing her gaze away from Frankie.

"The look of a woman desperate to get some lovin' from her man," the other woman said with a wink.

Annie shrugged. "With my ribs, it's been a while," she said simply.

"And he probably refused to do anything that he thought might hurt you," Aspen added, with uncanny insight.

"Yeah," she said with a nod.

"I love how he looks at you. As if the sun rises and sets with you. That man loves you desperately, Annie. He'd do anything for you," Rayne said.

"I know," Annie whispered. "I feel the same about him."

"Maybe the next time we all get together, it'll be for your wedding?" Aspen probed.

For once, Annie didn't get stressed out or irritated when someone brought up the question of when she and Frankie were going to get married. She'd had her reasons for wanting to wait, but now all she could think about was making this man hers for good. "Maybe," she agreed with a small smile.

Aspen beamed.

They were interrupted by Fletch calling for everyone to gather around him and Doug, as he wanted to give a speech. There were groans and moans, as Fletch's speeches were legendary for going on and on and being overly sappy, but the women all stood up and went to find their men anyway.

Frankie appeared out of nowhere the second Annie was standing. He led her over to where her dad and Doug were standing and stood behind her, his arms wrapped around her belly.

As Annie leaned against Frankie and listened to her dad embarrass the hell out of her brother, she couldn't help but smile. She'd missed this. Hanging out with people who knew and loved her. Seeing kids run around, laughing and smiling. Fletch had unearthed her old battery-powered tank that his friends had made for her years ago, and while it was looking a bit tattered, it still ran perfectly. Even the teenagers were getting in on the fun, wanting their turn to zoom around the yard.

If she decided to get out of the Army, Annie didn't have to think too hard about her dad's suggestion of looking into med schools in Texas. She wanted to be near her family. Near this chaos and love. It was one of the main things she'd missed about moving around the country and constantly being gone on missions.

"I love you," Frankie whispered into her ear.

Tightening her hold on his arms around her waist, Annie swallowed hard. She was lucky, and she knew it. She was healthy, had a patient man who loved her, and more people in her corner than she could count. It was easy to get bogged down in the everyday frustrations of life and not see the big picture...but Annie's big picture became a little clearer with every hour she spent with family and friends.

CHAPTER EIGHT

It's beautiful, Frankie signed as the shuttle bus pulled up to the pier in Barbados.

As much as he loved Annie's family, he was glad to finally be here. The last week had been full of laughter and love, and he was glad to see Annie somewhat relaxed after talking with her dad. He'd known Fletch wouldn't be upset that his daughter was thinking about switching careers, but he was relieved their conversation hadn't completely stressed her out.

As for Frankie and Annie, they'd had a long talk about what the future might hold for them and where they'd live if she did give up her commission. Annie wanted to leave it completely up to him; he didn't really care *where* they ended up, as long as they were together.

She finally admitted she wouldn't mind being close to her family, which again, wasn't a surprise to Frankie. When they got back from their vacation, she'd have a lot of thinking to do. Decisions to be made. If she was going to get out of the Army, she needed to research medical schools in Texas and what it would take to be accepted. If she was going to stay in, she'd put her energy toward training a new team.

He wasn't surprised she'd considered him when thinking of what their future might look like if she got out, mentioning veterans' hospitals in Texas and even engineering companies. He'd reassured her that he wanted to stick with what he was doing, helping people who'd lost their hearing acclimate to their new world. Frankie himself had worked hard to learn how to read lips, and his cochlear implant gave him the ability to hear, but because he'd been older when he'd gotten the implant, his speech was markedly different from that of others. He read the lips of people making fun of him all the time.

Shoot, I wish one of the fancy rooms had been available, Annie signed. Because they'd decided relatively recently to take the trip, everything had already been booked. There'd been a last-minute cancelation, and they'd been lucky enough to snag the very last room. It was on the same level as the bridge, where the captain and his officers steered the ship. The more expensive rooms were below the walking deck and were twice as big as their own.

But Frankie would live in a tent as long as he was with Annie.

Our room will be fine, he reassured her. *Doesn't matter if it's a closet, as long as I'm with you, I'm happy.*

Annie smiled at her man. *This* was why she wanted to change careers. So she could spend more time with the love of her life. Frankie never failed to make her feel good. He could make her forget all her problems.

Their guide stood up on the bus and explained the process for checking in and getting their keys. Annie and Frankie shuffled off and got in line to board the beautiful old sailboat. She could feel Frankie at her back, one of his hands on her hip. Normally she hated having people behind her, but not Frankie.

"Where are y'all from?" the woman in front of them asked, making small talk.

"Georgia right now, but we might be moving to Texas," Annie said with a smile.

"Oh? What do you do?"

"I'm in the Army," Annie told her.

She could see a change come over the woman's face. Her welcoming smile faded. "Oh, and your husband?"

"We aren't married," Frankie told her. "Engaged. I'm a house husband. You know, I keep the house clean, cook, do the shopping, that sort of thing."

The woman blinked, gave them a fake smile, then turned back around.

That was mean, Annie signed to Frankie. *You should've told her what you really do.*

She's a stuck-up bitch, Frankie signed back. *All she really wanted to know was if we were someone she should suck up to.*

She knew Frankie was right. She'd gotten a negative reaction in the past from people who heard she was in the Army, and never really understood why. It made no sense to her. Some of the most intelligent people she knew were in the armed forces. Doctors, scientists, engineers...and they were all doing what they could to keep the country safe. Feelings toward people in the military had come a long way since the 1970s, but there was still some sort of stigma about soldiers and sailors that Annie didn't understand.

They shuffled forward in the line and got checked in without any issues. They were given identification cards and escorted to their room by an employee wearing a crisp white uniform. As they passed other guests on the way, Annie could tell this cruise was going to be unlike anything they'd done together in the past.

As soon as the door shut behind them, Annie sighed. "We don't fit in."

"So?" Frankie asked.

Annie wasn't surprised he'd noticed the same thing. The other passengers were older and, judging solely by all the designer clothes and jewelry, of more means. Their jeans and T-shirts certainly made them stand out.

"Annie," Frankie put his hands on her shoulders, "who cares about the other passengers? I don't care what they do for a living or what kind of houses they live in. *Nothing* makes them better than us, and nothing makes them more entitled to this vacation."

"You're right," Annie said.

"I know," Frankie responded smugly.

Their plan had been to explore the ship, check everything out, see where the dining room was and greet their fellow passengers, but at the moment, Annie had no desire to hang out with anyone else or be polite. She'd rather be alone with her fiancé.

She stepped into him and rested her head on his shoulder, then grabbed his butt with her hands and squeezed. "We're finally alone," Annie said seductively.

She felt his chest rumble under her cheek before he asked, "How're your ribs feeling?"

Annie looked up and met his gaze. "They're fine. *I'm* fine." Frankie had always been protective of her, refusing to do anything that might exacerbate her various injuries over the years—including making love to her before she was completely healed.

He smiled. "I love your family. I love that you have such a huge support system. But visiting them doesn't leave us much time to ourselves, and I have to admit that I feel weird even *sleeping* in the same bed with you while we're there."

Annie grinned. "I know. I feel the same. Even though we're adults and engaged, I feel as if I revert back to being seven years old again when I'm around Dad and his friends."

Frankie ran a hand over her hair, then rested his palm on the back of her neck and squeezed lightly.

Annie shivered in anticipation. Looking at them, no one would guess that in the bedroom, Frankie changed from a mild-mannered, slightly nerdy guy who was happy to fade into the background to a man who took complete control. Who preferred to call the shots as far as their lovemaking went.

Annie never thought she'd be the kind of woman who would like that sort of thing either. But after spending her days making decisions and having everyone look to her for direction in life-or-death situations, she gladly gave up the reins to Frankie when it came to sex. She wasn't exactly submissive, didn't think she'd ever be able to sit back and let anyone, even Frankie, make every decision for her. But in bed? Absolutely yes. Frankie had never let her down. Not once. He was observant and attentive, and always made sure she came first. Every single time.

She had no one to compare Frankie to, but she'd heard stories from the men and women she'd commanded over the years. Knew that Frankie was somewhat unique when it came to his intense need to satisfy her even before meeting his own needs.

Frankie looked over his shoulder at the bed behind them. Two twin mattresses had been pushed together to make a slightly smaller-than-queen-size bed. There was about a foot of space on one side, while the other was flush against the wall. At the foot of the bed, where they were standing, there was only about three feet to spare. The room was...cozy. There were two windows on one side of the wall and a small bathroom with a shower. Their suitcases hadn't been delivered yet, and Annie knew once they put all their things away, the room would be quite full.

While a larger, more opulent room would've been nice, Annie no longer cared. She had two weeks of one-on-one time with her fiancé on this ship. She couldn't wait.

One hand still on her neck, Frankie reached for the hem of her shirt with the other, slipping underneath. His palm eased upward, covering one of her breasts possessively. He squeezed both hands at once, and Annie shuddered in anticipation.

She moved her hands to the front of his jeans and fumbled with the button.

"No," Frankie said in a low, rumbly tone.

Annie's hands froze, a slight whimper escaping her throat.

Frankie smiled lazily as he nudged the cup of her bra aside and twirled a finger around her nipple.

Annie closed her eyes and sighed, arching her back, wanting more. So much more. She felt Frankie's mouth on the sensitive skin of her neck as he nuzzled her, her body beginning to ready itself for him.

Just when his hands morphed from teasing to a more serious touch, there was a loud knock on their door and a voice called out, "Housekeeping. Your suitcases have arrived."

Annie jerked in surprise in Frankie's grasp, and he murmured, "Easy, love." Then louder, he called out, "We'll be right there!"

"It's like being in my dad's guesthouse," Annie grumbled. "Always afraid someone's gonna interrupt us."

Frankie smiled and leaned down to kiss her lightly. "Two weeks," he reminded her. "We've got two weeks all to ourselves."

Annie smiled as his thumb brushed back and forth on the sensitive skin of her neck. "I'm thinking we'll be headed to bed early after dinner."

"Oh, yeah," Frankie agreed fervently.

Annie shivered when he resituated her bra and his hand slipped out from under her shirt. She stood where she was as Frankie went to the door. The housekeeper brought in their suitcases and with the three of them in the room, and their two large duffle bags, there was precious little space left.

Annie did her best to get her libido under control as

the housekeeper explained the activities for the rest of the day and how they would be casting off the dock in about an hour, with dinner being served at seven o'clock. The man welcomed them once more, then finally left.

As much as Annie wanted Frankie, the mood had been broken.

"What do you want me to do to help?" Frankie asked.

Annie smiled. Her man knew her so well. Knew she preferred to both pack and unpack their things. She liked having everything in its proper place, even on vacation. Frankie was perfectly capable of putting away his own belongings, but since the room was so small, he knew without having to ask or being told that it was easier for Annie to handle it her way.

"You want to go see if you can find me a cup of coffee or tea while I get started? And maybe something sweet?" she asked.

"You got it," Frankie said without hesitation. He picked up the bags and put them on the end of the bed for her. Then he kissed her and headed for the door.

After it had shut behind him, Annie stood there for a long moment, relaxing into the silence. For the first time in ages, she realized she felt truly content. While she loved the Army and everything she'd accomplished, it wasn't until right this second that she realized how stressful her life had become. Not because she was worried she couldn't do her job, but because it took her away from Frankie so much.

She'd grown up without him, had gone to a different university than he had, and even since getting engaged and living together, she hadn't spent nearly enough time with him. But this two-week trip could be the start of a very different life together, and Annie was nearly giddy with the knowledge that while she'd still work long hours if she went into the medical field, and there would be days she regretted not being able to spend with him, the dangerous deployments could soon be a thing of the past.

Smiling, she turned to the first duffle bag and got started.

Frankie put his hand on Annie's thigh and squeezed, hard. They were at dinner, sitting at a table with two other couples. The seating was open, meaning anyone could sit anywhere they liked. As there were only sixty guests, the dining room wasn't huge; it was cozy and doubled as the library. Bookshelves lined the wall, full of novels about the Caribbean, pirates, and beautiful coffee table books with colorful pictures of island life.

At first, things had been cordial between the six people at the table. Dottie and Joseph were from Vermont, and he was a lawyer. Megan and Bill were from California. Frankie wasn't exactly sure what they did, but it had something to do with imports and exports. After some not-so-subtle questions and probing, it was obvious the couples were surprised that he and Annie could even afford this trip.

It was true it wasn't cheap, but they were frugal with their money. Annie made a good salary, especially with all her deployments and hazard pay. Frankie was genuinely surprised at how concerned their table guests were with their financial status, but then again, he spent most of his time around down-to-earth people like his and Annie's family and friends...and the soldiers he worked with at the VA. In his opinion, everyone should be concentrating on the fact they were in paradise on vacation, not worrying about how their fellow passengers could afford space on the ship.

Frankie could ignore the fact that they were being judged by these strangers, but he hated that they seemed to look down at Annie's job. It was obvious they were uncomfortable with his disability as well. The room was loud, with everyone talking at once. While his implant gave him the ability to hear, in situations like this, he was overwhelmed by the noise level. He could read lips, but the couples frequently turned their heads or looked down when they spoke, making it difficult to understand them. He had to ask them to repeat their questions several times, which was obviously irritating them quickly.

Frankie didn't care what these strangers thought of him. He'd experienced his fair share of discrimination over the years; stares and nasty comments didn't even faze him anymore. But Annie *hated* it. He'd had to step in more than once and stop her from going off on someone for making a snide comment or saying something out of ignorance. He suspected she was on the verge of ripping into these hoity-toity assholes. Hence, his current tight squeeze on her thigh.

When she turned her head to look at him, Frankie's suspicions were confirmed. The anger in her eyes and a slight flush meant she was about two seconds away from losing her cool.

He did the one thing he knew would get her attention.

I want you.

Frankie used to feel bad about using sign language around others; it was akin to talking behind their backs. But he'd gotten over that pretty quickly. It came in handy when he wanted to talk to Annie, his dad, or his godparents without anyone knowing what he was saying.

"You can't be serious?" Annie said out loud in surprise.

Frankie smiled. He'd successfully distracted her from whatever she was about to say to the other couples at the table. Knowing they were watching, and not caring in the least, Frankie signed once more. *You don't often wear a dress, and you look absolutely beautiful tonight. I can't wait to get you back up to our room and see what you're wearing under there.*

I know what you're doing, Annie signed back. *You're trying to keep me from leaping across this table and telling these assholes how offensive they're being and that if they don't stop looking down their noses at us, they're gonna go cross-eyed.*

Frankie chuckled.

"Um, we missed the joke," Bill said.

"Yup," Annie said without looking away from Frankie. *If everyone else on this ship is like them, I'm gonna jump overboard and swim home.*

No, you aren't, Frankie told her. *You hate swimming.*

Fine, you can do the swimming. I'll lay in a floatie behind you and you can tow me.

I'm sure not everyone is as stuck-up as they are, Frankie reassured her.

Annie gave him a skeptical look.

"It's cool that you guys can talk to each other like that," Dottie trilled, not sounding as if she thought it was cool at all. "Although it's kind of rude since we can't understand you."

Annie turned to her, her eyes practically sparking, and Frankie held his breath.

"*Rude?* You telling my fiancé that he speaks 'pretty good for being deaf' was rude. As was wrinkling your nose when you heard I was in the Army. I'm sorry my profession isn't good enough for you. But because of the things *I've* done in the military, you're able to sit here today, enjoying a delicious dinner with the money your husband has made. My job keeps *you* safe, keeps terrorists from going through with their plans for another 9/11. And if you don't like not knowing what we're saying? Try living your entire life as a deaf person. Or blind. Until Frankie got his cochlear implant, he struggled to communicate even his slightest needs to the hearing community. Learning sign language isn't hard. There are plenty of Internet sites that will teach you the basics."

She took a breath to continue, but Frankie interrupted. "We're sorry for excluding you from our conversation," he said. "We're so used to talking to each other with our hands that we sometimes forget others don't understand us." He was lying through his teeth, but forged on. "We were talking about how good the meal was tonight, and how amazing the chef has to be to cook dinner in the tiny kitchen we saw as we were walking around earlier."

Dottie's cheeks were bright red. Frankie had no idea if she was embarrassed—rightly so—or if she was pissed, but since she was looking anywhere but at the two of them, he figured it was probably the former.

The others at the table nodded and agreed with him

about how delicious the meal was, and Frankie internally sighed in relief. He didn't care what the others thought about him, but he also didn't really want to spend the next two weeks tiptoeing around the boat, hoping to avoid these couples.

The waiter appeared at their table to refill everyone's wine glasses, which was impeccable timing, as far as Frankie was concerned.

She's a bitch, Annie signed.

Frankie did his best to keep the smile off his face, but he wasn't all that successful. Annie was right, but he figured it was best to try to smooth things over. "So, Joseph, what was your most memorable case? Or can you tell us?"

It was the right thing to ask. As they finished their meal, Joseph went on and on about some of his more prestigious cases, according to him. He used no names, but Frankie actually laughed a few times at his descriptions of his clients and some of the things they'd done.

Frankie and Annie both declined dessert and were the first ones to leave the dining room. The second they stepped out onto the deck, Frankie sighed in relief. The din of everyone talking was muffled as the door shut behind them. Putting his hand on the small of Annie's back, he relaxed when she leaned into him. Instead of going straight back to their room, they wandered over to the railing. Annie snuggled into him, her back against his chest as they watched the water churning against the sides of the boat as they sailed to their first island destination.

"Excuse me."

He tightened his hold on Annie instinctively as he turned to see who'd spoken.

One of the sailors on the ship stood there, looking nervous. "I don't mean to interrupt, but I heard you were deaf?"

Frankie felt Annie stiffen in his arms. "I am," he confirmed. "I got a cochlear implant years ago, so I can hear as long as I'm wearing the external device," he explained as he turned and pointed at the device on the side of his head, behind his ear. "I can also read lips, so if there's an emergency I won't be a liability."

The sailor shook his head and smiled apologetically. Then he shocked the hell out of Frankie by signing, *My sister is deaf, but I haven't seen her for over a year. I miss her, and I'm afraid I'm getting rusty with my signing. I was just hoping that maybe I could practice with you while you're onboard?*

Annie stood up straighter in his arms. *Of course you can,* she signed, beaming at the young man. *What's your name?*

Manuel.

I'm Annie, and this is Frankie.

Are you deaf too? Manuel asked.

Annie shook her head. *No. But I realized a long time ago that if I wanted to talk to the guy I love, I needed to learn.*

Manuel nodded. *I didn't mean to bother you. I just got so excited when I heard there was a deaf person onboard, I couldn't wait to find you and talk to you.*

Anytime you want to have a chat, I'm happy to, Frankie told him.

Thanks. We're kept pretty busy around here, but I'll take you up on that if you really don't mind, Manuel said.

I don't mind at all, Frankie said.

Manuel nodded at them. "Have a good night. It's supposed to be smooth tonight and conditions are looking good tomorrow for sailing," he said out loud.

"Do you go up in the rigging?" Annie asked.

Manuel smiled. "Yup. I go all the way up. I'm responsible for the top lines and sails."

"Wow, brave."

The young man shrugged. "Always did like climbing trees when I was little. Enjoy your night." Then he walked away.

Just when I'm ready to jump overboard and hate everyone, someone has to come along and change my mind, Annie signed.

Frankie smiled. His Annie was passionate about everything she did. When she liked someone, she expressed it with her whole heart. When someone disappointed her or was rude, she didn't hesitate to make her displeasure known. He felt her relax against him once more and was grateful to Manuel for helping to calm her down.

"What time is it?" she asked, tilting her head back and looking up at him.

Frankie smiled. He loved being out in the fresh air, watching the water race by as they stood on this beautiful sailboat, but at the moment, all he could think about was taking Annie back to their room and showing her how much he loved her. No one stood up for him like she did. No one was as big a champion for him as she was. He was a damn lucky man, and he knew it.

He wasn't rich. Would never be the most popular or handsome man in a room. He'd always have struggles because of his disability, but Annie had never, not once, made him feel as if he was worth less because of who he was or what he did for a living. If anything, she was responsible for him having a healthy self-esteem. From the time they were kids to now, she constantly told him how amazing, smart, good-looking, and strong he was.

It's time for me to see for myself if you're healed or not, he told her, desire filling him.

He felt the instant change in her demeanor. Her body melted into him as she smiled. "Yeah?" she asked.

"Uh-huh."

"I'm *completely* healed," she said seductively.

"It's gonna take a pretty thorough exam for me to make sure," Frankie replied.

Annie beamed, then grabbed his hand and turned. She towed him behind her as she headed for the stairs that led to their room.

Frankie laughed and allowed himself to be led. He'd follow this woman wherever she wanted to go. No questions asked.

CHAPTER NINE

Frankie closed and locked the door behind him and stared at Annie. He hadn't lied at dinner. She looked absolutely breathtaking tonight. She had on a simple sundress with spaghetti straps. The black dress with yellow flowers had a tight bodice, before billowing out at her hips and falling just above her knees. The skirt was loose and flowy, and his hands itched to strip her bare.

His Annie was breathtaking. Her body was muscular and toned, but she was still all woman, curvy in the right places. She frequently complained that her thighs and butt were too big, but Frankie wouldn't change one thing about her. It didn't matter if she weighed one hundred pounds or three hundred, he'd never love her any less. He was aware some men would insist he was missing out, since he hadn't been with any other women, but Frankie knew they were wrong.

The only woman he'd ever wanted, *would* ever want, was the one standing in front of him right now.

As if a switch had been flicked inside him, Frankie

stood straighter as he stalked toward her. He could see Annie's pulse beating in her neck. She wanted him. Needed him. Maybe even more than he needed her at the moment. He'd purposely kept his hands to himself over the last month while she healed. Trying to make love to her when she had broken ribs would have been too painful. It hadn't been easy for either of them, but if there was one thing he'd learned during her years in the military, it was that anticipation made their lovemaking so much more intense.

"Go ahead and use the restroom," Frankie said. They'd lived together long enough for him to know she preferred to get ready for bed first. Annie went up on her tiptoes and kissed him gently, then turned and headed for the small bathroom in their stateroom.

Frankie went to the bed and pulled back the covers, then took off everything but his boxers. He put his dirty clothes in one of the duffle bags Annie had stored away, then turned off all the lights except for the one beside the bed. He wished he'd thought ahead and purchased some pretty flowers or something, anything to make the room less...austere. But he knew Annie wouldn't care, let alone hold something like that against him.

Before too long, Annie appeared from the bathroom. She wore the oversized T-shirt that she liked to sleep in and her cheeks were pink with anticipation. God, he loved her. She was just as beautiful and enticing in an old T-shirt as she'd be if she were wearing a sexy nightie. She didn't have to try to seduce him; she did it just by being herself.

Smiling at her, Frankie headed into the bathroom to brush his own teeth. He considered taking off the external device of his implant but decided he wanted to hear every sigh and moan that came out of Annie's mouth. He'd take it off before he went to sleep.

He left the bathroom and joined her under the covers, sighing in contentment when Annie immediately snuggled up next to him. She put her head on his shoulder and wrapped an arm around his chest.

"There's nowhere I'd rather be than right here with you," Frankie said after a moment.

He felt her soft sigh caress his chest. "Same," she replied. Then Annie propped her chin on her hand and met his gaze in the dimly lit room. "I hate that others have all these preconceived notions about you just because of your implant and the fact that you're deaf."

Frankie shrugged. "You know I don't care."

"I *do* know," she said with a frown. "But people like those judgmental assholes at dinner still piss me off so bad."

"If I lived my life constantly worried about what strangers thought of me, I'd be a hot mess," Frankie told her. "The only people who I care about are our friends and family. As long as they're proud of me, I'm good."

"I'm proud of you," Annie said immediately.

Frankie smiled. "I know you are."

"And I know that you're smarter than eighty percent of the population," she added.

"Only eighty percent?" Frankie teased.

Annie shrugged. "There are always those people like Brain and his son, you know, the ones who are super, *super* smart. You're just super smart," she joked.

"I can live with that," Frankie said. "I love you. No one's ever made me feel as wanted and appreciated as you."

"Not even Jenny?" Annie asked quietly.

Jenny was a girl he'd known his entire life back in California. They were in the same class since the first grade, and she'd always had a crush on him. Annie didn't like her. There wasn't a good reason for her feelings, since Jenny had always been perfectly nice and never overstepped, but Frankie understood. Growing up, Annie was unhappy that Jenny was always around him, at school together day after day, and she wasn't. Her jealousy was a real thing, and no matter how many times Frankie assured her that he'd never felt anything beyond friendship for Jenny, he hadn't been able to shake her dislike of the other girl.

"Not even Jenny," Frankie said solemnly.

Annie sighed again and put her head back down on his shoulder. "I know I'm being ridiculous. But she got *so much* of your time. All I can say is that it's a good thing she didn't go to the same university you did. I'm not sure I would've been able to handle it."

That was another plus for Annie, as far as he was concerned. She wasn't afraid to come right out and admit her shortcomings. Jenny had always been a sore spot with her, and she knew it.

Not wanting to talk about another woman while they were in bed, even if it was someone he hadn't seen in almost a decade, Frankie ran his fingers gently up and down Annie's arm. Her skin was silky smooth and he knew at the end of their two-week vacation, she'd be tan and hopefully the stress lines by her eyes will have disappeared. He planned on pampering his woman and enjoying every second of their down time. Being together for two weeks straight, neither of them having to work and without the constant threat of her being called out on a mission, was absolute heaven.

As eager as he was to make love to Annie, he was enjoying this. The intimacy. The closeness. Just talking to her about nothing. "You looked like you were having a good time at your parents' house."

Annie nodded. "Being around my mom and Fletch seems to recharge me somehow. Them and their friends. They're all so much in love, even after all these years."

"They are," Frankie agreed.

"And even though their get-togethers are crazy, they're so much fun. I can't wait to see what shenanigans everyone gets into at our wedding."

Frankie momentarily tensed, then forced himself to relax...but Annie didn't miss it.

"What? What's wrong?"

"Nothing," Frankie soothed.

She frowned up at him, then closed her eyes for a moment and shook her head. "Jeez, I'm an idiot," she said quietly.

"No, you aren't," Frankie countered. He hated when she put herself down, even if she was kidding.

Annie came up on an elbow next to him and put a hand on his cheek. "I am. I talked to my dad about this, and my mom, and even some of the other women...but I never said a thing to you, which is awful. Frankie...I'm ready. I want to set a date. Get married. Fletch said we could have the reception at their house, if that's okay with you. He promised he'd even post guards so there wouldn't be a repeat of what happened at his own reception."

Frankie swallowed hard. *This.* This was what he'd wanted since he was seven years old. To marry Annie. He'd done as his godfather had suggested, given her space. Never tried to pressure her into anything she wasn't ready for. He would've waited his entire life, and if she'd never wanted to make it official, that would've been okay.

But seeing his Annie walking down an aisle toward him? Pledging to love him for as long as they both shall live? It would literally be a lifelong dream come true.

"Frankie?" Annie asked, the worry easy to hear in her tone.

He rolled until she was under him, then gazed down at her adoringly. "Having the reception at your parents' place is perfect," he told her. "I love you so much, Annie. I always have. I've never really understood why you chose me, but I'll make sure you never regret it."

Annie grinned at him. "My mom's gonna go overboard," she warned.

"Don't care."

"You're going to have to wear a tux. And super-polished black shoes. And because I don't have any close friends, she's already suggested I have all *her* friends be bridesmaids."

"Fine."

"Which means their husbands will probably be your groomsmen."

"Annie, you and your mom can arrange for forty-seven people to stand up with us, and I still wouldn't care. As long as you're by my side, anything else won't faze me."

"You say that now," Annie said with a roll of her eyes. "Fletch already talked about retrofitting that tank of mine to hold our rings and he wants to roll it down the aisle when it's time."

Frankie laughed. He wouldn't put it past Fletch to do just that.

"And I'm sure my mom's gonna want to put those stupid Army men in with the flower petals thrown in the aisle. I'll probably trip over one."

Frankie couldn't stop smiling. He'd seen the pictures and heard the story about how Annie had snuck her precious plastic Army men into her basket when she was the flower girl for her mom and Fletch's wedding. "Probably," he agreed.

Annie took a deep breath. "We probably should just go to the justice of the peace or Vegas or something."

Frankie shook his head. "No way. You're everyone's favorite, and you know it. You would devastate everyone if you did that. Truck would probably cry. And no one wants to see the big bad Truck bawl like a baby."

Annie grinned. "True. I don't know how long it'll take to plan this wedding though," she warned.

Frankie got serious. "It doesn't matter. One month, two...three years. It won't change my commitment to you. When I asked you to marry me, I promised to love you forever. For better or worse, for richer or poorer, in sickness and in health. That hasn't changed, Annie. If anything, I feel it even stronger. I don't need a big fancy ceremony to prove my love for you, but I know how much that day will mean to your family. So I'm happy to do whatever it is you, and they, want. But at the end of the day, when it's just the two of us like we are right now, I want you to fall asleep knowing what's most important—that you have a man who will always put you first. Who will do anything to keep you happy and content. Who will guard you with his very last breath if that's what it takes."

"Frankie," Annie whispered, clearly overwhelmed.

"You have no idea how amazing you are. You don't see the way other men stare at you with lust. I know you think you're a little weird and not very womanly, but you're so wrong, it's not even funny. I'm awed that you're with me, and I'll never take that for granted. I love you exactly how you are, weirdness and all. I love that your idea of fun is to run through an obstacle course on whatever Army post we're near, with a bunch of kids trailing behind. You've got such a beautiful soul, Annie, and I treasure you so damn much."

"Okay, stop talking," she pleaded. "I still feel stupid that I talked to everyone but you about our wedding. That was so rude."

Frankie laughed. "You could surprise me with my own wedding, and I wouldn't be upset about it. But I want to help in any way I can. If you want to let your mom plan everything, fine. If you want to get involved, great. I'll look over books of wedding invites and go with you to pick flowers and taste cake all you want. I just want you to be happy, love. That's all."

"I am," she reassured him. "But..." Then she began to wiggle under him, and Frankie frowned in confusion, lifting off her a bit to give her room. When she shrugged out of her shirt, lying naked under him, Frankie took a long moment to study her.

She was beautiful all the time. But naked? She took his breath away.

"Less talk, more action," she said sassily.

Frankie was all for that. "Close your eyes," he ordered.

She immediately did as he requested.

It slayed him that Annie let him control their lovemaking. She'd admitted more than once that because she made the tough decisions with her teams, it was freeing to not have to take the lead in their bedroom. And conversely, Frankie was so laid-back in his everyday life, it felt empowering to take the reins when it came to sex.

Telling himself to take things easy because of her ribs, even though it had been so damn long since he'd made love to his woman, Frankie took a deep breath. He planned on showing her exactly how much she meant to him. And if it drove them both crazy in the process, all the better.

Ever so slowly, he bent and kissed her collarbone. Then the pulse hammering in her throat. He moved down her body, worshiping as he went. He placed a kiss on her belly, loving how she inhaled deeply. She was ticklish, and it was just one more thing he loved that he knew about her, that no one else did.

Gently easing her legs apart, Frankie kissed her inner thigh. Then the other one. He looked up her body, and saw he had Annie's undivided attention. Good.

Determined to make sure she enjoyed this, he closed his eyes and got to work pleasuring the woman he loved more than he could ever express.

Annie woke up the next morning feeling completely relaxed. It had been a very long time since she'd had nothing pressing she needed to get up and do. She didn't need to go to PT. Didn't need to think about what meetings she'd be attending that day. Didn't have to worry about being called in to post or sent on a mission.

Stretching lazily, she realized that she was alone in bed. Opening her eyes, she saw Frankie standing near the bathroom, gazing at her. Blushing as she remembered their lovemaking from the night before, Annie smiled. "Morning."

"Morning, beautiful," Frankie said.

"What are you doing?"

"I'm watching you," her man said without hesitation. "And pinching myself that you're mine."

Every now and then, Frankie would say something that reminded her so much of her dad and his friends. They never hid their love for their wives, and she freaking *adored* that Frankie was the same way. She also loved his dominance in the bedroom. It was such a turn-on, and last night had been no different. He'd taken his sweet time, kissing and caressing every inch of her body before making gentle, slow, sweet love to her.

Then, once he was very sure she wasn't feeling any pain from her most recent injuries, he'd taken her again, hard, rough. Morphing into the dominating, forceful, wild lover she knew he could be.

"You're mine as much as I'm yours," Annie said.

"Absolutely. I thought I'd go and grab you something to eat in bed this morning. You know, just to make sure you didn't have another run-in with Dottie or Megan and their husbands. Wouldn't want to start your day off on a sour note."

Annie grinned. "Sounds awesome. How much time do we have until the sailors climb the rigging to raise the sails?"

"Johnny said they'd try to do it around nine."

Johnny was the guy in charge of the guests on the ship. Annie supposed he was a cruise director of sorts. Even though this was a small vessel, someone still had to organize everything and make sure the passengers were happy.

Glancing at the clock, Annie saw it was seven. Very late for her on a normal day, but she was feeling extremely lazy. "Since someone kept me up late last night, I might sleep for another hour or so," she told Frankie.

He moved then, coming around the side of the bed. He put one hand on the mattress and leaned down to kiss her. "Stay in bed as late as you want. Today's a sea day. There's nothing we have to do, and I'm sure you'll get to see the sails being put up and down many times in the next two weeks."

A slow start in bed sounded amazing. "Okay."

"Okay," Frankie echoed. "I'm headed downstairs. I'll bring up coffee for you, and a plate of fruit or something."

"Thank you. Don't let anyone give you any shit," Annie told him.

"I can handle the others, don't worry."

But she did. Annie constantly worried about Frankie. Not because she didn't think he could take care of himself, but because the thought of anyone looking down on him made her completely crazy. Always had.

Frankie kissed her once more on the forehead before

he straightened. Today, her man was wearing a short-sleeve green shirt and a pair of board shorts. He looked relaxed and happy.

"Love you," he said as he headed for the door.

"Love you too," Annie echoed.

He smiled at her before she heard the door click shut behind him. She heard him talking to someone in the hall, and she figured he was probably telling housekeeping that she was still inside sleeping. That was her Frankie. Always so considerate, always looking out for her. Letting her sleep in when she could, getting her breakfast, leaving her small love notes around their house, and a million other things.

Annie had been so busy in the last year, training new men on her team and trying to make sure everyone stayed alive on their missions, she realized she'd become less aware of the things Frankie did for her. The laundry was always done and folded when she got home. He cooked. Cleaned. Took the trash out every week. Mowed the grass, paid their bills, and picked up birthday cards for all her pseudo cousins. And he did all of it while still working himself.

He wasn't perfect. He always left lights on, which made her nuts; she was constantly turning off lights in his wake. He rarely watched one show at a time, constantly flicking between channels instead of just watching a program all the way through. The DVR was full of shows he recorded but never watched. And it *really* annoyed her when he was in a bad mood and removed his speech processor, then refused to look at her so she couldn't communicate with him. It was something a three-year-old might do, but he did it very rarely, thank goodness. Still, it drove Annie crazy.

But she could absolutely deal with all his minor faults, because she had just as many. He was so good to her, and Annie knew she'd never find anyone she trusted more. She and Frankie had shared so much growing up. They sent letters and talked online as much as their parents would allow it. He was truly her best friend, and she was his.

Annie grinned and stretched, feeling erotic aches and pains she hadn't felt in too long. Yeah, it was safe to say that she was keeping Frankie. Forever.

An urgency to marry him swept through her. They'd put it off for so long, the intensity of her need to be Mrs. Annie Sanders wasn't too surprising. She wanted to tie herself to him so tightly, he'd never be rid of her. It was a small miracle he'd stuck by her for so long, given the challenges of her career. She wouldn't risk losing him now. Not that she thought she would, but a small bit of fear was always there, in the back of her mind.

Knowing her mom, she'd have the entire wedding planned by the time Annie and Frankie got back from their vacation. The thought wasn't objectionable.

Annie curled onto her side and pulled Frankie's pillow into her embrace. She inhaled deeply, bringing his musky scent into her lungs. Closing her eyes, she let herself drift off into a light doze, completely content.

CHAPTER TEN

The days were going by quickly. A week had passed in the blink of an eye. Almost every day, the ship stopped at a different small island in the Caribbean. Annie wasn't much for swimming or snorkeling in the ocean, so they opted for exploring the islands on foot. Sometimes going with a group on the planned activities, other times heading out on their own.

They'd eaten in local restaurants, joined a pickup game of soccer while walking by a small school one day, saw ancient ruins and forts. Annie couldn't remember a time she'd felt so carefree. Certainly not since she'd joined the Army.

The trip helped her realize all the more that getting out was the best decision. She was proud of what she'd accomplished, but she wanted more than traveling from country to country, trying not to get killed while simultaneously trying to kill others. She wanted to build a life with Frankie, spend time with her family, and just enjoy the future in general.

Despite a number of seemingly superior or just plain rude passengers on the ship, they'd met a few others who were more down-to-earth. They'd managed some pleasant conversations over lunches and dinners with some of the guests. Manuel and Frankie had also spent time together, and Annie could see that even after those relatively brief visits, Manuel had lost some of his rustiness, the signing coming easier each time.

Today, the plan was to go to a large uninhabited island in the Bahamas, the one she'd mentioned to her mom's friends. Annie wasn't sure of the name, only that the cruise company owned the beach on the south side of the island. While most of the guests were excited for today's stop, because the beach was absolutely picturesque, Annie much preferred the islands with towns and cities so they could interact with the locals and find out-of-the-way cafes to enjoy. She liked to experience the different cultures.

Johnny promised that the snorkeling was unparalleled at the beach and the turquoise water made for some beautiful photo opportunities. Annie had tried to persuade Frankie to go snorkeling with the group, but he refused, saying he'd rather spend his time with her.

And since Annie didn't enjoy swimming, that was that.

Luckily, Johnny said there was also a hike through the rainforest on the island that guests could take. It was only a mile round-trip, however, and while the heat and humidity were pretty intense, Annie was itching for a more vigorous workout. She hadn't been able to run like she was used to, and while she was nearly certain she'd be telling her commander she was getting out of the Army when her reenlistment came up, she wasn't out yet.

Therefore, she needed to stay in shape. It was highly likely she'd be deployed at least once before then, maybe more.

The passengers had to wait their turn to board the smaller Zodiacs ferreting them to shore, but Annie didn't mind. She had no problem letting the more impatient guests crowd the first few boats. By the time it was their turn, she was already sweating. It was three o'clock in the afternoon and the sun was still high in the sky, the rays beating down on them as they raced toward shore.

When they got to the beach, most of the guests were already in the water snorkeling or lounging in the sun, working on their tans.

"The last boat leaves at five," Manuel told them. He'd been one of the sailors assigned to bring passengers to and from the sailboat.

No problem, Frankie signed back to him.

"Have fun!" the other sailor on the Zodiac said. "Since it doesn't look like you're dressed to swim, the hiking path is just over there to the right. It snakes through a portion of the jungle and spits you out at the other end of the beach. You can either walk back on the beach, or turn around and go back through the jungle. There's a fork about half a mile down; be sure to turn left."

"Where does the other path go?" Annie asked, curiosity eating at her.

"Eventually to the north side of the island, but the path isn't straightforward, nor is it maintained. There are a lot of twists and turns and it's easy to get lost. So make sure you turn left at the fork. You wouldn't want to get left behind," the sailor advised.

"I don't know," Frankie said with a small laugh. "It's pretty damn beautiful."

"True. But you'd get sick of eating coconuts soon enough," the guy said with a smile. "Besides," his voice lowered, "you don't want to get snatched up by pirates. Or run into any secretly bred dinosaurs that might look cute but are totally deadly, would you?"

Annie burst out laughing. "Are you referencing the second *Jurassic Park* movie? Where that fancy yacht goes to an island and the young girl gets attacked by the compies... those little dinosaur things?"

"Sure am," the sailor said with a wink. "So be sure to stay on the path."

"We'll be careful," she told him breezily as she tugged on Frankie's hand. "And if we see any dinosaurs, we'll be sure to let you know."

The sailor chuckled and waved them on. Annie was itching to get going and out of the hot sun. Being in the forest wouldn't help lower the humidity, but at least they'd be in the shade for much of their hike.

She heard Frankie chuckling behind her as she towed him toward the path.

"In a hurry?" he asked

"Sometimes I forget how much people annoy me," Annie teased.

Frankie only laughed harder. "I wonder how many people they've lost out here?" he mused.

"My question is, if they didn't want people going across the island to the other side, why does the path fork in the first place? They should've built a new one that doesn't even have the option of taking a wrong turn."

"Good point," Frankie said, squeezing her hand.

Minutes passed in silence as they walked through the forest, before Frankie said dryly, "Can we not walk at a forced-march pace though?"

Annie immediately slowed her steps. "Sorry," she said with a wrinkle of her nose "It's just really nice to stretch my legs and get some exercise."

Frankie stopped abruptly and pulled her into his arms. Annie would've been annoyed because they were both pretty sweaty already, and he knew she wasn't a fan of touching anyone while working out, but his hold immediately reminded her of the night before. The heat they generated in bed...how he'd been relentless in making sure she was deeply satisfied before he considered his own needs. She'd heard enough bedroom horror stories from other women to realize how good she had it with Frankie.

"Breathe, love," he told her. "We're on vacation. Not storming the beaches of Normandy or heading to a Taliban hideout."

"I know," she sighed. "I just need a good workout."

Frankie raised an eyebrow and smirked as Annie realized what she'd just said. "I mean, the workout I got in our bed last night was good, but—"

He kissed her abruptly. "I know what you meant. Let's just slow down a bit and see where this path leads us. If we need to walk it several times to get the itchiness out of you, we will."

Annie smiled. "Have I told you today that I love you?" she asked.

"Yeah, but I'll never get tired of hearing it," he said.

"I love you, Frankie. I don't understand how you put up with me sometimes, but I appreciate it all the same."

"You're not so bad," he told her with a wink. "Even if you do hog the covers, leave your shoes all over the house, and you burn water."

Annie laughed. "Why don't you lead? That way, we can keep this a nice relaxed hike rather than a super-extreme workout."

"You could run on ahead and come back and meet me," Frankie suggested.

Annie shook her head. "No. I'd rather stay with you. I'm on vacation. It's not going to kill me if I don't run a million miles with a thirty-pound pack on my back."

"You aren't going to get out of shape," Frankie reassured her.

"I know. And anyway, I'll miss things if I go first. You're so good at pointing out birds and interesting-looking bugs and stuff."

"Okay. But if I go too slow, just let me know."

They started off again, this time with Frankie in the lead. He kept their walk at a semi-leisurely pace, stopping often to check out cool plants and flowers.

Annie had no idea how much time had passed, but it wasn't long before they came upon the fork in the path they'd been warned about.

Frankie stood in front of it, looking to the right—where they clearly weren't supposed to go—then to the left. Someone had strung a flimsy rope across the path to the right. Annie looked at it longingly. She could see a slight rise through the trees in the distance, which would be a slightly better workout, and she couldn't help but think it would be just a little more thrilling to explore the forbidden path.

"You know, they did say the island is uninhabited," Frankie mused.

Annie grinned as she looked at him. "They did," she agreed.

He looked at his watch. "And we have plenty of time. Especially if we picked up our pace. We could go see this other beach and still make it back for the last Zodiac to the ship."

"Since when did you get so adventurous?" Annie asked.

"Since I've been with you," Frankie said without hesitation.

"We're supposed to stay on the left path," she reminded him, not sure why she was making even a token effort to talk him out of the off-limits trail. She definitely wanted to go to the right.

Frankie shrugged. "I'm feeling a little rebellious today, what I can I say?"

"I like it. And if that other beach is deserted...maybe we can see if beach sex is all it's cracked up to be," she said, grinning.

Frankie's eyes got wide. "Um...no. I love you, but getting sand on my dick isn't high on my list of things to experience. Besides, that shit could be highly irritating for you too. Can you imagine having to go to the ship's doctor and explain why you have a nasty rash on your hoo-ha?"

Annie burst out laughing, but she nodded. "Okay, okay, you're right."

"If we had a towel, maybe," Frankie went on. "And I'm not willing to risk finding leaves and shit to lie on because with my luck, there would be some huge deadly spider that would bite my ass. Then *I'd* have to explain to the ship's doctor how some tropical spider managed to get inside my shorts and underwear and bite me."

Annie almost couldn't talk, she was laughing so hard. "I said all right!" she managed to choke out.

"I love seeing you laugh like this," Frankie said fondly.

"Come on, before you get me all hot and bothered with your sexy talk of sand and spiders," Annie dead-panned, grabbing his hand once more and tugging him off the path so they could walk around the rope blocking the trail.

"Oh, you're hot all right," Frankie quipped.

Annie rolled her eyes. Her man was a dork, but she wouldn't have him any other way.

They walked on, and Annie loved how it felt as if they were the only ones on the island. The birds were chirping overhead and the leaves blew in the slight breeze. The earthy smell of the dirt and sand under their feet just added to the ambiance.

The trail they'd chosen had branched off several times. Some of the tracks they followed were little more than animal paths, but Annie wasn't afraid of getting lost. For one, they were on an island; there was only so far they could roam. And two, she'd always had an excellent sense of direction. She knew she could get them back to the beach on the other side of the island without any issues. But she could certainly see how others might get lost.

"It's so beautiful," Annie said after they'd been walking for a while.

"It is," Frankie agreed from behind her. She'd taken the lead once more.

"How much time do we have?" she asked.

Frankie looked at his wrist. "We're still good," he said. "We've been walking less than an hour."

"Okay." Annie lifted her head and inhaled deeply. "Smell that?" she asked.

"Yup. We must be getting close to the other side of the island."

Annie nodded in agreement. The smell of the ocean was stronger. They'd gone up and over a ridge that was probably dividing the island into its north and south sides. While the south side, where the boat had anchored near its private beach, had calm water and only a slight breeze, the north was much more wild and windy.

One second they were surrounded by trees, and the next they were standing at the entrance to a long stretch of beach. Annie internally nodded at her earlier assessment. This side of the island wasn't as suited for tourists lying around and relaxing. And definitely wasn't ideal for snorkeling. The surf was rough, pounding onto the sand. The beach itself was very rocky, nothing like the long blanket of soft sand found on the other side of the island.

But for some reason, Annie liked this beach better. It was rougher, more real. "It's beautiful," she breathed.

"It is," Frankie agreed.

Annie carefully walked down the beach, taking it all in. The wind whipped the strands of hair that had escaped her ponytail, stinging her cheeks and neck, and she could feel the salt in the air coating her skin. Inhaling deeply, she couldn't help but smile. She felt more alive in this moment than she had in a very long time.

Frankie was about ten feet behind her, taking his time as he studied the area. Neither spoke, simply enjoying the serenity of the moment and the beautiful scenery.

About halfway down the beach, Annie saw something ahead of her, close to the tree line. She couldn't figure out what she was seeing. It looked like a bunch of crates...but that made no sense. They were completely alone and the island was uninhabited, so what the heck was she seeing?

She walked a little faster, eager to solve the mystery. When she got within twenty feet or so of the mysterious containers, she froze in her tracks.

A man suddenly stood up from behind the crates just inside the trees—and for a brief second, they simply stared at each other. It seemed the man was as surprised to see her as she was to see him.

Instinctively, Annie took a step backward. There was something about this man that had the hair on her arms standing up. He had blond hair and a very scruffy beard, as if he hadn't shaved for a week or more. His shirt was dirty and his shorts torn. He looked...nervous as hell. A lot like the people she'd seen on missions who were trying to blend into their surroundings, but were much too keyed up and nervous to convince anyone they were going about ordinary, everyday business.

But it was what he held in his hand that had her turning toward Frankie.

She had every intention of demanding he run—but Frankie was already racing toward her.

Annie's gaze flew back to the man they'd surprised, but

before she could do more than register he wasn't where she'd last seen him, he was suddenly beside her, the gun in his hand now shoved against her head.

"Don't move," he growled.

Annie froze. She wanted to disarm this asshole, but on the slim chance she failed, she didn't want to think about what he'd do to her or Frankie. She also had no idea if he was alone or not. She needed more information before she made a move.

"What the hell?" Frankie yelled as he got close.

"Don't come any closer or I'll shoot her!" the guy yelled.

Frankie ignored him and continued to run toward them.

"I mean it!" the man warned.

"He's deaf!" Annie shouted.

"What?"

"He's deaf!" she repeated. "He knows sign language. I can tell him what you're saying, but I have to move my hands. Please don't shoot me." Annie worried she was overacting a bit too much, but if this asshole didn't know Frankie could actually hear, that might work in their favor.

"Tell him to fucking stop!" the guy said, nudging her head with the muzzle of the pistol.

You should've run the other way, Annie told Frankie.

Frankie stopped ten feet from where she stood. *You think I was going to leave you? No fucking way,* he signed back.

Even though he wasn't speaking, Annie could see his irritation loud and clear in the way he signed.

"I thought this island was uninhabited," she told the asshole.

"You thought wrong," he responded. "There are a few dilapidated old cabins on the north side, not too far from here. As far as we can tell, someone came over from Nassau, probably squatting on the island." The man lowered his voice, muttering, "Of all the fucking islands, they had to pick this one."

We. That answered the question about whether the asshole was alone or not. And he was American. He had no accent that Annie could discern.

"Look, just let us go and we'll go back to the other side of the island," she said softly. "We don't care what you're doing here. We're on vacation. We don't want trouble."

"Well, you found it anyway," the man said. "We can't let you go and blab to someone about us being here. And we can't shoot you because the assholes in the cabins might hear and come investigate. Not to mention, I'm assuming you arrived on that fancy fucking boat. *Those* assholes might hear gunshots and come looking too. So for now, you need to be all quiet like and do what I say."

"What the fuck's going on, Garrett?" another man asked as he came out of the tree line, stomping toward them.

Annie's stomach dropped. Shit. The asshole—Garrett—had already given away the fact that he wasn't alone on the island, but Annie had hoped his partner was sleeping or something. She could easily take one guy, but two would be harder. And the second man was also carrying a gun. *Shit shit shit.*

"We've got company," Garrett said.

"No shit, Sherlock," the man said in disgust. He walked up to Annie, leering as his gaze roamed her body.

"Leave her alone," Frankie said in a hard tone.

"Is he retarded?" the second guy asked after hearing Frankie's voice.

Annie saw red. "No, he's not retarded! And that's the most offensive fucking word in the English language."

"He *sounds* retarded," Garrett argued.

Annie tensed, ready to kill both of these men.

Easy, Annie. Stay focused, Frankie signed.

"What's he doing? Having a seizure?"

"He's deaf," Garrett informed his friend. "Or so she says."

"He is," Annie affirmed. "He sounds different because he can't hear himself. It's impossible to learn how to sound out words when you haven't heard them first. If someone gave you a book written in French or Spanish or any other language, you'd sound pretty weird when you spoke too."

"Huh. So he can't hear us?" the second man asked.

"No."

"And you talk to him with your hands?"

"Yes," Annie clipped.

"Tell him to get his ass over here and sit behind the crates," he ordered.

Don't do it, Annie told Frankie. *If you turn around and run, you'll surprise them and have a head start. They might not be able to catch up. You can go back to the other beach and get help.*

I'm not leaving you, Frankie said, his lips twisted into a deep frown.

Annie loved her man so damn much, but at the moment, she was frustrated by his stubbornness.

"What'd he say?" Garrett asked.

"He wants to know what you guys are going to do to us," Annie lied.

"If you do what we tell you to do, nothing," the second guy said. "We've only got another day on this shitty island before we're picked up."

What's the plan? Frankie asked.

I don't know yet, Annie told him. *They don't sound like they want to kill us. We probably need to just wait them out.*

Not want to kill us? That asshole has a gun to your head, Annie!

"What's he saying?"

"He wants to know where you want him to sit. And what's in the crates." Annie wasn't sure she really wanted to know. But if there were guns, she could maybe get into one and even the odds a bit.

"Should we tell her, Travis?" Garrett asked, his voice mocking as he kept the gun pressed against her head and Frankie slowly walked toward where they'd told him to sit.

Travis followed him. "You want to know what's inside our crates?" he asked.

Annie didn't know if he was deliberately being an ass or if he'd forgotten Frankie supposedly couldn't hear. She guessed it was the former. *Don't react,* she warned Frankie as he glanced her way. But deep down, she knew he was the more tolerant of the two of them. If anything, she was telling *herself* not to react instead of Frankie.

"Cocaine," Travis said succinctly. "We're gonna be fucking rich as soon as this shipment gets picked up. We're here to personally make sure the delivery goes off without a hitch. Our guys are coming down from Miami to get us and the shit."

Annie tensed. Damn.

"Sit there," Travis told Frankie, waving his gun at him, using it to point to the ground next to one of the crates. Garrett had walked her around the crates, where she saw the two men had made a small camp of sorts farther into the forest. There was a small fire pit and trash thrown everywhere. Two hammocks were strung between trees and a large jug, which Annie assumed held water, sat off to one side. What she *didn't* see was any other weapons. She'd been hoping to get her hands on one.

Garrett took hold of her arm and yanked, almost making Annie fall to the rocky ground. Frankie made a noise in the back of his throat and started to rise, but Travis brought his pistol up and pointed it at his head. "Sit back down," he threatened.

I'm okay, Annie told Frankie.

Garrett laughed. "Looks like it'll be easy enough to keep you both compliant. How about this: I'll shoot you if he steps out of line, and if you do the same, he's dead. Tell him that."

Garrett nudged her with the muzzle of his pistol and hatred rose up within Annie. *This* was why she'd wanted Frankie to run. If he was safe, she'd do whatever was needed to take these fuckers out. But she had no doubt they'd shoot Frankie if she so much as twitched. She had to let these assholes think they had the upper hand. For now.

"Tell him," Garrett repeated, shoving his gun against her skull harder.

We need to wait them out. They'll need to sleep eventually,

Annie told Frankie. *Stay calm and don't give them a reason to get pissed at us.*

They're underestimating me, Frankie said.

I know. And we can use that to our advantage. But not right now, when they're on high alert.

Frankie nodded and sat back against the crate.

"Good boy," Garrett cackled. Then he led Annie over to a tree on the other side of the makeshift camp and shoved her to the ground. Annie fell to her knees and bit back the groan that threatened to escape when her knee hit a sharp rock. If Frankie thought for one second that she was hurt, he'd lose it. If shit hit the fan, he'd die trying to protect her. It didn't matter that she was a Special Forces soldier. It didn't matter that she could take care of herself.

Frankie had never forgotten how it felt to be helpless when his own mother had tried to kidnap him when he was a kid. He had a huge savior complex now, and most of the time Annie didn't mind. It felt good when he stood up for her...but now wasn't the time for him to lose his head.

I'm okay, she told him for what seemed like the hundredth time.

If he doesn't get his fucking hands off you, he's gonna lose them.

We just need to stay calm, she repeated.

"If he moves, shoot him," Travis told Garrett as he leaned over a bag.

"What about the sound traveling? People coming to see what's up?" Garrett asked.

"Fuck," Travis swore. Then he shook his head. "We'll just take that chance." He turned to Annie. "I suggest you and your friend here stay very quiet. You won't like what happens if you don't."

It was a tad reassuring that they hadn't *already* shot them, that they were worried about drawing attention to this side of the island.

Then Travis stood up, a length of rope in his hands, and any sense of reassurance fled.

"As Garrett said, as long as you sit there like a good little girl, and your friend does the same, you'll be fine. Tomorrow, our friends will be here to pick us up and you'll be on your own again. In the meantime, I can't have you running off on us," Travis said as he squatted beside her.

He expertly tied one end of the rope around the tree, the other around Annie's waist, securing it with a series of complicated knots. "I'm gonna leave your hands free so you can translate for your retarded friend."

Her teeth clenched. "Stop saying that. He's as smart as anyone else. Smarter."

"Yeah, right. He sounds pretty stupid," Travis muttered, tightening the rope around her.

Annie sucked in a breath. "That's too tight," she whined.

"Shut up, bitch," Travis told her, but Annie was relieved when he loosened her binding just a bit.

Then the psycho drug dealer turned and punched her right in the face.

She grunted with the force of his fist connecting with her cheek. It hurt, but she'd been through much worse pain in her path to becoming a Green Beret.

Garrett and Travis laughed.

"Tell your boyfriend that if he, or you, tries anything,

you'll get much more than that. You aren't my type...but it's been a while since I've sunk my dick in a pussy. You'll do. Tell him that," he said, punctuating his order with a kick to her thigh.

I'm fine, Annie told Frankie, who she could see was on the edge of losing control. *He hits like a pussy.*

I'm going to fucking kill him, Frankie said.

He wants you to lose control, Annie sighed quickly. *I'm seriously all right.*

Frankie nodded, but she could see he wasn't happy. Not at all.

Annie's adrenaline was sky high and she wanted nothing more than to tackle this asshole, but she needed to play it smart. And time was her friend right now. They were supposed to be back on their ship soon. When they didn't show up, surely the captain would look for them. All she needed was for the captain to call the Bahamian authorities for assistance. Once that happened, it was only a matter of time before they'd be found.

Annie knew without a shadow of a doubt the cavalry would be called in. She and Frankie just needed to be patient and not antagonize Travis or Garrett until then.

"What'd he say?" Travis asked.

"He wants to know what you're going to do next," Annie made up on the fly.

"Whatever we want," Travis said, emphasizing his point with his pistol. "Tell him that."

I love you, Frankie, Annie told him. *We're gonna get through this.*

I'm sorry I suggested taking that damn trail, Frankie said.

Annie shook her head. *You know I would've talked you*

into it.

True. Then, proving they were on the same wavelength, he said, *Only about an hour before we're supposed to be back. They're gonna look for us.*

"What the hell's he saying?" Garrett asked.

"He's just scared," Annie said. "As am I."

"Tell him to shut up. Jesus! Who would'a thought a deaf guy could be so irritating by talking so much?"

We need them to let down their guard. Help is gonna come, but if we can do something before then, we will.

Tell me what to do and I'll do it, Frankie told her.

Annie nodded. God, he was such a good man. Didn't even hesitate to let her know he would follow her lead. They both knew she was the expert when it came to this kind of situation, and even though Frankie would die for her, he was willing to let her do her thing to get them out of this.

Her love for him almost overwhelmed her in that moment...before the seriousness of their situation finally hit home.

Frankie could die today.

Annie wasn't afraid of death. She'd stared it in the face so many times, it barely fazed her anymore. But the thought of something happening to Frankie nearly paralyzed her. She couldn't lose him. Couldn't imagine a life without him.

And with that thought, determination rose within her.

She *wasn't* going to lose him. Not to these assholes.

For now, we wait, she told Frankie.

He nodded, then lowered his head as if they were beaten.

CHAPTER ELEVEN

Frankie sat against the crates filled with drugs and tried to come up with a plan. But strategizing was Annie's forte. All *he* could do, really, was remain complacent so neither of the men hurt her. He'd glanced at his watch earlier and saw that it was well past the time they were supposed to have been back at the beach. The captain and the other employees surely knew they were missing by now.

They were probably scouring the beach and the trail for them. He had no idea what would happen when they weren't found quickly. Hopefully they'd widen the search.

Some of the other guests onboard would be pissed that their vacation was being interrupted. That they hadn't left for their next destination. A few of the people they'd met would be concerned. They might even volunteer to help search. But it was going to get dark soon, and Frankie didn't think the cruise line would want paying guests tromping around the forest in the dark. Probably wouldn't even want their own employees doing so.

That was okay with him. Frankie didn't want anyone else to stumble on Garrett and Travis. He had a feeling they wouldn't hesitate to shoot anyone who dared get in the way of delivering their drugs.

Annie was right, they just had to lie low. Not antagonize the men with the guns.

For the last hour or so, Travis and Garrett had sat a short distance away from him, talking. They kept their weapons at the ready, but as long as he didn't make any sudden movements, they seemed content to ignore him.

He'd learned quite a bit from them already, since they thought he couldn't hear. And every piece of info he learned, he'd passed on to Annie. At first the men had demanded to know what he and Annie were talking about. She lied through her teeth, making up enough stupid shit that they'd stopped asking. Which was a colossally dumb move on their part. They should've known they'd be discussing how to escape. But instead, they mostly complained about the bugs and discussed how much money they were going to make when they got the crates back to the States.

They're brothers, Frankie told Annie. *Travis is older. They're worried about their dealer getting impatient. If their friends are late picking them up, the deal could fall through.*

Not our problem, Annie said.

It might be if they get jumpy about it, Frankie countered. *It would be best if we weren't here when the other drug guys show up.*

I agree. We can wait until the middle of the night. Hopefully one or both of them will fall asleep and we can sneak away.

Frankie liked that she wasn't hell bent on capturing the two men. He much preferred to get the hell out of there and let the authorities take care of the brothers. Not that he didn't think Annie could do it, but they'd have to split up while one guarded the men and the other went back to the other beach for help. The absolute last thing Frankie wanted to do was separate from Annie.

Hours went by, darkness fell, and Frankie ignored the rumbling of his stomach. He was hungry and thirsty, but every muscle was taut, waiting to see what the men might do with them.

"What if they don't show?" Garrett asked his older brother.

"They will," Travis said.

"But what if they don't?" Garrett insisted.

They were speaking softly again, secure in the knowledge that Frankie couldn't hear them. For the first time in his life, Frankie was glad he was deaf. It was working in his and Annie's favor.

"They're gonna come," Travis said, the irritation easy to hear in his voice.

"What are we gonna do with *them*?" Garrett asked.

Frankie tensed as he waited for Travis's response.

"We'll see what Martin wants to do."

Garrett chuckled. Frankie might've thought the younger brother was a little naïve and not as dangerous as Travis, but his next words belied that thought.

"He won't want any witnesses that can ID us or tell someone what happened here. Think he'll let me do it?"

Frankie stiffened.

What are they saying? Annie asked impatiently. She was

obviously not happy that she couldn't hear the brothers firsthand.

Give me a second, he told her, straining to hear Travis's answer.

The older brother shrugged. "I don't see why not. He's not going to care *who* kills them, as long as it gets done. You're gonna have to shoot them in the head, kill them immediately so we don't make more noise than necessary. Make the shots count. Make sure they're dead. We don't want anyone finding us before we can get off this stupid island."

"I can do that," Garrett said almost excitedly. "Maybe we should just do it now so Martin doesn't have to worry about them. He'll be pleased if he gets here and we've already taken care of business."

"Good point," Travis said. "But we need to wait a bit, because I'm sure there are people from that ship out looking for them. They'll eventually come to this side, but probably not until daylight. They'll concentrate on the south side first, along that trail they made. We've got some time. If we do it now, they might hear the shots. We can handle a couple of squatters, but not a whole damn ship crew."

"What if they find us before Martin gets here?" Garrett asked.

"They won't."

"How can you be sure?"

"Because! Now shut up!" Travis told his brother. "All we have to do is keep our heads down until our pickup. We'll be in the clear then."

Frankie wanted to roll his eyes. They had to know

someone from the ship could show up at any point, night-time or not. It was probably smart not to make any unnecessary noise to pinpoint their location, but eventually the entire island would be searched and they'd be found. There was no way they had until morning, whenever their buddies were showing up. They were delusional if they thought they did.

"All right, but I still think we should take care of them before Martin gets here. It'll make him happy, and prove that we'll do whatever it takes and can handle the responsibility of working with him. We can bring their bodies with us and throw them overboard once we're far enough out to sea. They'll never be found, and no one will ever trace them back to us."

"Good idea," Travis agreed, nodding slowly.

New plan, Frankie signed to Annie. *As soon as we get a chance, we need to take it.*

Why? What are they talking about?

They think the guy coming in the morning will want us dead. Garrett is eager to make his first kill. They decided it would be better if they shoot us before their partners come.

Shit.

Yeah. But they want to wait a little longer, hoping the shots don't alert anyone looking for us.

Okay, that will give us some time.

I'll see if I can get a hold of the knife Travis used earlier and cut the ropes holding you to the tree before they know what I'm doing, Frankie told Annie. He had no idea *how* he would accomplish that, but he'd do whatever it took to free her. Even if it meant getting shot in the process.

No need. I'm already free, Annie said.

Frankie blinked in surprise. *You are?*

Yeah. Asshole doesn't know the first thing about how to properly secure someone, and he shouldn't have left my hands free. We just need to be ready to take them out the first time they let down their guard.

Frankie had what seemed like a thousand questions. He had no idea how Annie had been able to get the rope around her loosened without their captors even noticing. He didn't know how they were going to "take them out" when Travis and Garrett had guns and they didn't, and he wasn't sure how they'd know when it was the right time to make their move.

Before he could ask any of that, something hard struck him in the forehead.

Frankie flinched with pain and immediately brought a hand up to his head. He could feel wetness.

"Perfect aim, Garrett!"

Frankie looked up and saw the brothers laughing. Garrett swung his arm back, preparing to throw another rock.

"Stop it," he growled.

"The retard speaks!" Travis crowed.

Frankie had been called a lot of names in his life, so the slur didn't even register. He'd worked very hard in the last twenty years to speak more clearly and to pronounce words correctly, but he'd always sound different from hearing people. He didn't care, because Annie didn't care. She'd done wonders for his self-esteem.

But he was also well aware how much Annie hated when people treated him badly or made rude comments about how he sounded. Before the situation got out of hand, he needed to do something. Knowing Annie wasn't helpless, wouldn't be a sitting duck against that tree if he pissed the brothers off, gave Frankie the courage to see if he couldn't move things along. He wanted Annie back on their boat, safe and sound. Away from these volatile drug dealers, and *definitely* before their buddies showed up.

"I need to pee," he blurted just as Garrett threw the second rock. Frankie ducked and it flew over his head, hitting one of the crates behind him.

"You missed!" Travis crowed.

"He moved! Wasn't my fault," Garrett complained.

"You're gonna have to have better aim than that if you're gonna hit him later," Travis said.

"Did you hear him?" Annie called out from across the way. "He said he has to pee."

Frankie kept his eye on the men, not wanting to get hit in the head with another rock. He had to believe Annie recognized, and approved of, his attempt to change things up. Now that they knew the brothers planned on killing them, they couldn't be content to just sit around and see what would happen next.

"I heard him," Travis snapped.

"We've been sitting here for hours," Annie went on. "You guys haven't given us anything to eat or drink, and you've pissed several times. Come on...please?" she whined.

"Fine. Garrett, you take him," Travis said with a shrug.

"Why me? You do it. I don't want to be alone with the retard," Garrett complained.

"Stop fucking calling him that! He's deaf!" Annie yelled. "Not mentally challenged!"

"Mentally challenged," Travis said with a laugh. "I guess that's the politically correct term for retard, huh?"

Frankie had a feeling if this conversation went on for too much longer, Annie was really going to lose it. So he said, "Please? I promise to be good. I don't want to get hurt." He did his best to sound as docile as he could.

"Fine," Garrett mumbled, standing. He pointed his pistol at Frankie. "Stand up."

Playing his role, Frankie stared up at the man and furrowed his brow as if he was confused.

"Fuck," Garrett said, as his brother laughed. "Stand up!" he yelled, as if that would somehow help Frankie hear him. He gestured upward with his hands, the pistol waving wildly in the air.

Frankie nodded and slowly stood, keeping his hands up as if in surrender.

"Tell him I'll kill you if he tries anything," Travis told Annie.

Don't listen to him, Annie signed. *This is good. We need to separate them.*

Frankie lifted his hands to respond, to ask what the plan was, but Garrett slammed his pistol against one of his hands.

Yelping in surprise and pain, Frankie glared at the man.

"No more talking!" he growled. "You wanted to pee, so that's what we're gonna do. Walk!" He pointed toward the trees beyond where they'd been sitting.

Frankie walked toward the trees, trying to think of what to do next. He had no doubt Travis would gleefully shoot Annie if given the chance. Even more horrifying was what the two men could do to her *before* they killed her.

He wasn't an idiot. Annie was pretty, and he didn't want to think about how these assholes might violate her if given the chance.

No way were they going to put their hands on his woman.

He kept an eye on Garrett as they walked a little ways into the forest. It was a good thing he actually did have to use the restroom. If he didn't, he had a feeling Garrett would lose his mind.

"There. Piss there," Garrett said, gesturing to a spot next to a tree.

Frankie nodded and reached for the fastener on his shorts. He did what he needed to and nodded at Garrett when he was done. It was hard to believe the brothers were so stupid, they hadn't figured out what the speech processor on the side of his head was. Even if they'd never met anyone who was deaf, they had to wonder what the hell he was wearing. Maybe his hair covered it enough that neither man had noticed.

"Go on, get back to the camp," Garrett ordered, once again gesturing back the way they came with the gun.

Frustrated that he had no plan in mind, and the opportunity hadn't presented itself for him to do anything, Frankie did as ordered and headed back to camp. He hated turning his back to Garrett, praying the other man wouldn't take the opportunity to shoot him right then and there.

Just as they neared the camp, Garrett called out to his brother. "I'll be right back. I'm gonna piss!"

"Whatever!" Travis yelled back.

Frankie didn't stop walking as he heard Garrett turn around and head back into the trees.

His heart rate increased. This was it. This was what they'd been waiting for. They wouldn't have a lot of time, but if they could get Travis subdued before Garrett returned, they'd certainly be able to overpower the second man.

Walking faster, wanting to give himself as much time as possible, Frankie steeled his resolve. Without giving himself time to think, he burst into the clearing and charged Travis.

The other man was still sitting on the ground, and he looked up a split second before Frankie tackled him.

"Ahhhhhh!" Travis yelled, and Frankie winced. He'd hoped to surprise the asshole enough that he wouldn't have time to yell out for his brother. At least his tackle had managed to knock the pistol out of his hand. Frankie saw it lying in the sand as he wrestled with the drug dealer.

Frankie rolled with Travis as he struggled to subdue the man. A sharp pain hit the side of his head. As if a switch had been thrown, Frankie's world fell silent. Travis had managed to knock the speech processor off his head. It was held on by a powerful magnet, but it wasn't hard to remove the device.

He couldn't hear anything for real now, and had no idea if Annie was trying to tell him anything or not. He didn't know if Garrett had heard his brother's yell and was even now racing back to the camp.

Adrenaline coursed through his veins, and Frankie looked up long enough to see Annie appear at his side. He read her lips as she said, "I've got him. Take care of Garrett."

Frankie rolled away from Travis without a second thought, trusting that his badass woman could handle the pissed-off drug dealer on her own. He had no doubt that if Garrett came into camp and saw what was happening, he wouldn't hesitate to start shooting.

Just as Frankie got to his feet, he saw Garrett. It was obvious the other man had heard his brother's cry and had come running, his gaze locked on Annie and Travis.

Frankie didn't hesitate. He'd never been the athletic type, but he'd watched his share of football games over the years. With nothing but the thought of protecting Annie screaming in his head, Frankie launched himself at Garrett when he cleared the trees. His shoulder hit the other man in the stomach and they went down. Hard.

Garrett was slender, but he was a fighter. Frankie had no idea what was happening behind him with Travis and Annie, but he couldn't concentrate on anything other than subduing the pissed-off man thrashing beneath him. Grabbing hold of Garrett's wrist, Frankie strained to keep the gun pointing away from him.

Just as he thought he had the upper hand, Garrett's finger curled around the trigger.

Frankie saw the flash of the muzzle, his opponent wincing at the sound of the gun firing.

Garrett got off a second shot—and Frankie saw red.

He had no idea where the rounds had gone, but he was scared to death one might've hit Annie. He wrenched the gun out of the man's hand and blindly threw it away toward the trees. Using all his strength, he punched Garrett in the face. Once. Twice. A third time.

Frankie had never hit anyone in all his life. He didn't like confrontation, avoided it at all cost. But something came over him in that moment, and he knew if he didn't end this here and now, he and Annie were in deep shit.

He saw Garrett's lips moving, but he was too lost in his rage to read the words. He kept punching the other man until he brought both hands up to his face to fend off Frankie's attack.

A touch on his shoulder had Frankie spinning around, ready to take on Travis.

It was Annie standing next to him.

Go watch Travis, she signed. *I'll finish this.*

Frankie looked beyond Annie and saw Travis lying motionless on the sand. He had no idea if the man was dead, but he wouldn't shed a single tear over him if he was.

Even before Frankie nodded, Annie moved. She barely gave him a chance to get out of the way before she flipped Garrett onto his stomach and began to hog-tie him with the same rope they'd used to tie her to the tree. She wrapped the rope around his wrists, then wrenched his legs up and tied his bound hands to his ankles.

Frankie ran to where he'd thrown the pistol Garrett had used, thankfully finding it quickly, and carried it over to the crates. Placing it on top of one, he turned back to help Annie. She already had Garrett completely under control.

He'd always known how amazing his woman was, but at that moment, it truly hit home.

She was currently dragging Garrett into the camp, near

his brother, without seeming as if it took any effort whatsoever. She was covered in sand and scratches from head to foot from wrestling with Travis and didn't even look like she was out of breath.

Frankie, on the other hand, knew he was breathing as hard as if he'd just run a 5K race at a full-on sprint. He could feel his heart pounding and knew if he could hear himself huffing and puffing, he'd be embarrassed.

Watch them. If they move, shoot them, Annie signed, then she went back to where he'd been wrestling with Garrett.

Frankie picked up the pistol again and did his best to hold it steady, his hands shaking. It was hard to believe their situation had changed so drastically in mere minutes. He had no idea what Annie was doing, but when she bent over and grabbed something from the ground, then started back toward him, he figured it out.

She was holding his speech processor.

They'd just had a life-or-death fight, and she not only knew the device had been knocked loose, but her first priority was to retrieve it for him.

Feeling dizzy, Frankie swayed, then backed up so the crates kept him upright, his eyes on Annie. He didn't move as she got close, reached for his head, then gently reattached the device.

The first thing Frankie heard once the magnet clicked into place was deep moaning.

His eyes flicked behind Annie and he saw Travis moving restlessly. His hands were also tied behind his back, his ankles shackled together. But it was the large red stain under his thighs that made Frankie blink in surprise.

"He was shot. One of the rounds that his brother got

off hit him," Annie said nonchalantly, as if she were talking about the weather.

Frankie's heart sped up again at hearing that. It could've hit her. *She* could be the one lying in the sand bleeding.

As if she knew what he was thinking, Annie put a palm on his cheek. "I'm fine," she said. "You were the one I was worried about. I thought he'd shot *you*."

Frankie shook his head. He couldn't speak.

"Hey! Help him!" Garrett called out.

Annie didn't even turn around. She lifted her hand from his cheek to his forehead and scowled at the small cut there from the rock Garrett had hit him with earlier. "Asshole," she muttered.

"Seriously! He's really hurt! He needs help!" Garrett yelled.

Frankie saw the look of irritation cross Annie's face a split second before she turned her head and said, "Maybe your friends will help him when they get here."

"He's gonna bleed to death before then!" Garrett protested.

Annie sighed and looked back up at Frankie. "You okay?" she asked quietly.

Frankie nodded.

Annie reached down and took the pistol from his hand and put it back on the crate behind him. Then, as if they both hadn't almost died and weren't covered in sweat and sand, she put her hands on Frankie's face and leaned in.

Not hesitating, Frankie met her halfway. He kissed her as if he hadn't done so in years. He'd almost lost her. If she wasn't so amazing, and hadn't been able to escape her bonds or subdue Travis, they both would've been killed. He knew it down to the marrow of his bones.

He'd take his Special Forces woman over anyone else in the world. She outshone him in so many ways, but he didn't give a shit. He loved that she was stronger, smarter, and more amazing than he was. He paled in comparison, and he had absolutely no problem with that.

CHAPTER TWELVE

Inside, Annie couldn't stop shaking. She'd learned over the years to control her outward reactions, but at the moment it was taking everything she had not to burst into tears. When she'd heard the gunshots, she'd thought for sure that Frankie had been hit.

She couldn't believe that he'd literally tackled both men. He hadn't hesitated, had run straight toward them as if neither was holding a damn gun. It was lucky that he'd been able to take them by surprise, otherwise he could've easily been shot.

"You're seriously just gonna let him lie there and die?" Garrett screeched from behind them.

Sighing again, Annie eased away from Frankie. She kept her hands on his face. He was holding her tightly against him, and the last thing she wanted was let him go to deal with the two assholes behind her.

Their taunts and slurs against Frankie were still fresh in her mind. They'd planned to kill them both, so why should she do a damn thing to help them now? What she really wanted to do was head back into the forest to the other side of the island, apologize for getting lost, and get back on their ship to continue with their vacation, leaving the brothers and their mess behind.

But too much time had passed. Wheels were already in motion, and if she wasn't mistaken, it wouldn't be too long before the cavalry arrived. Hopefully before the drug runners did.

"I am so damn proud to be yours," Frankie said softly.

"I think that's my line," she responded.

He shook his head. "Nope. You're definitely the head of our family. I'm in awe of your strength and abilities."

Annie smiled up at him. "We make a good team," she said.

"A team's only as good as their leader," Frankie retorted.

"Come on, man!" Garrett begged.

"He's not so arrogant or mean without his gun, is he?" Frankie asked with a shake of his head.

Knowing she needed to deal with those jerks, that she couldn't let Travis bleed to death in the sand even if he deserved it, Annie caressed Frankie's cheek lovingly once more, then took a deep breath and turned to face the men who had every intention of killing them before the night was over.

The beach was dark, but light was coming from a lantern near where Frankie and the brothers had been sitting. There was also a full moon in the sky above their heads, giving her a bit more ambient light to see with as well.

Annie sauntered over to where the brothers were

trussed. She stood over them with her hands on her hips. "Wow, look, Frankie. He looks pretty bad. Garrett's right, he'll probably bleed out in less than an hour."

"Huh. That's too bad," Frankie said, following her lead as she knew he would.

"Wait—I thought he was deaf?" Garrett said in confusion. One cheek was lying on the rocky sand, his face beat all to hell from Frankie's thrashing. He wiggled a bit, trying to get loose, but Annie had tied him too tightly.

"He is. He has a cochlear implant," Annie replied.

"A what?"

Annie rolled her eyes. "Basically a really strong hearing aid."

"So he can hear us?"

"Yup."

"He heard *everything* we were saying?"

"Yes."

"So what was with all the sign language shit?" Garrett asked.

"We were plotting against you," Annie said succinctly.

"Fuck!" Garrett swore.

Annie simply laughed.

"You know, you could probably help Travis out," Frankie said conversationally.

"Probably," Annie agreed.

"Yes! Help him!" Garrett pleaded.

"Why?" Annie asked.

"Because! Otherwise he'll die!"

"You were going to kill *us*," Annie argued. "You were gonna shoot us in the head and dump our bodies in the ocean where no one would find us. You looked forward to it, in fact. So why should I do a damn thing to help either of you now?"

For once, Garrett had nothing to say.

"She's a medic," Frankie informed Garrett. "In the Army. In fact, she's a Green Beret. You know what that is?"

"I've seen the movie *First Blood* with Stallone. She's no more a fuckin' Green Beret than Kermit the Frog is," Garrett said. "They don't allow chicks in their ranks."

Both Annie and Frankie laughed.

She squatted down in front of Garrett. "You're an idiot," she said without heat. "I don't give a shit if you believe my man or not. But the fact remains, I kicked your brother's ass and hog-tied you both before you could blink. And if you want my help, you might try *not* pissing me off. Haven't you ever heard the phrase, you can catch more flies with honey than vinegar?"

Annie wasn't surprised when Garrett looked confused. "Whatever. Just patch him up enough to make it until our friends get here. They'll help him."

"Your friends aren't going to save you. They aren't going to get these drugs, and your guy back in Miami is most definitely gonna be pissed with all of you when he doesn't get his shipment."

"You don't know that," Garrett said gruffly.

"I do," Annie said, smiling. "See, here's the thing. My dad is former military. As are all his buddies. And he's got this really amazing friend who's a computer nerd. A hacker, if you will. When Frankie and I didn't show up to catch the boat back to our ship, the guy in charge of the guests probably sent out a search team. When they didn't find us, they would've reported back to the captain of our ship. He, in turn, would've contacted the Bahamian authorities, since we're in their jurisdiction.

"The second our names went into a computer, an alert would've sounded back in Pennsylvania—alerting my dad's computer geek friend. I have no doubt whatsoever he called in as many markers as he could to find us. So even now, as your brother slowly bleeds to death—from the bullet that *you* shot him with—teams of very pissed-off men are on their way to this island. To find me and Frankie.

"Like I said...I don't give a shit if you don't believe I'm Special Forces. You underestimated me once, and look what happened. But you'll definitely shit your pants when the cavalry arrives. They'll confiscate these crates, then they'll lie in wait for your druggie cohorts to get here and arrest them too. You're fucked, Garrett. If I were you, I'd be a little nicer so I help your brother before he bleeds to death."

She stood up and crossed her arms over her chest, waiting for his response.

Every muscle in Garrett's body sagged. He wouldn't meet her gaze. "Please. Help him. He's all the family I have left."

Annie wanted to refuse. Wanted to tell him to fuck off. But that wasn't who she was. "I'll help him on one condition."

"Anything," Garrett said.

"When the authorities get here, you cooperate fully. You tell them everything. How you found this island, how long you've been using it to smuggle drugs, the names of whoever you got the drugs from, who your friends are, who your contact is in Miami...*Everything*."

"They'll kill me," he whispered.

"Maybe. Maybe not," Annie said. "But if you want your brother to have even a chance to live, you'll agree."

Garrett was silent for a while, and Annie felt Frankie move up behind her. He put one hand on the small of her back and she leaned against him just a little. She wasn't feeling as brave as she was trying to look, and having Frankie at her back gave her the confidence to stand her ground.

Just then, Travis moaned.

It was the motivation Garrett needed.

"Fine. I agree," he mumbled.

It was Frankie who squatted down next to the hog-tied man then. "She wasn't lying about her dad and his friends. She'll tell them what you agreed to, and if you go back on your word, you'll *wish* you were dead."

Annie couldn't help but smile. God, she loved Frankie. He claimed he wasn't very alpha, but at that moment, he was just as scary as any Special Forces soldier she'd ever met.

Garrett nodded in response.

Annie mentally sighed in relief. It was killing her not to do anything to help Travis. Even though he'd had every intention of hurting her and Frankie, it went against everything in her to let someone suffer.

She kneeled in the sand by Travis and unwrapped the rope she'd tied around his ankles. He was in no condition to fight her, simply moaning as she jostled him. She tied the rope around his thigh in a simple tourniquet, then she pressed her hands tightly against the wound. The bullet hadn't hit a major artery. If it had, he would already be dead, but he wasn't out of the woods by any stretch.

Frankie stood nearby, waiting for her to tell him how to assist, but at this point, all that could be done for Travis was to stop the bleeding. He needed a hospital. Annie was confident she could at least keep him alive until help arrived.

And she hadn't lied to Garrett. She had no doubt Tex's programs had pinged when she and Frankie were declared missing. And she also had no doubt he had enough former and current military connections to get to them. It was just a matter of when.

She didn't know how much time had passed before she heard a sound over the wind and crashing of the surf. She'd gotten Travis's bleeding stopped, but the man was definitely in need of more advanced care than she could give him at the moment. He was currently lying semi-conscious in the sand.

Garrett had stopped begging for them to remove his bindings. He'd claimed everything under the sun—from circulatory issues and asthma, to anxiety and even diabetes —to try to convince them to untie him, but Annie and Frankie had ignored all his whining. He wasn't getting untied. Not by them, at least.

Glancing out at the ocean, Annie struggled to find whatever had made the noise she'd heard. Standing, she picked up the pistol while Frankie turned off the small lantern. There was every possibility these could be the brothers' druggie friends coming to pick them up.

If it was, they were early, and Annie and Frankie were in deep shit.

Crouching behind the crates, Annie strained to see who was approaching. Holding her breath, she prepared for a fight. She wasn't going down easy. She and Frankie had managed to make it so far, she wasn't giving up now. No freaking way.

Frankie didn't ask questions that she had no answers to. He didn't bitch about their situation. He was a rock. *Her* rock. He'd been amazing. No, he wasn't a Green Beret, and he hadn't had any problem with her taking charge of their situation, but when the time was right, he'd acted without hesitation.

Determination rose within Annie. She wasn't going to die and wasn't going to let anything happen to Frankie. They had their entire lives ahead of them, and no asshole drug dealers were going to take that away.

Suddenly, the decision she'd been struggling over on whether or not to stay in the Army seemed like a no brainer. No job in the world was worth a minute more than necessary away from the man she loved.

Her fingers tightened around the pistol and she saw Frankie do the same with the weapon he held. They were ready for whoever might be in the fast-approaching boat. Annie could see it now. It was a black Zodiac, much like the ones she and their fellow passengers used to go from the ship to shore and back again.

The boat didn't slow as it came in hot. It barreled right toward the beach as if whoever was driving had a death wish.

When the operator shut off the engine at the last

second and the boat smoothly but quickly glided onto the sand...Annie knew without a doubt that they'd been rescued.

She was proven right when six men exited the boat, three on each side, fanning out in perfect formation. She was ninety-nine percent sure no random drug dealers would be that confident driving a boat or so precise in their movements.

But just to be safe, Annie stayed where she was for a beat longer.

"Captain Fletcher?" a voice called out. "Sergeant Billings here. We see you behind the crates. Are you hurt?"

Annie closed her eyes as she heaved out a huge relieved sigh. She started to stand, but Frankie grabbed hold of her biceps.

"They might be bluffing."

She could hear the stress in her man's voice. "How would those druggies know we're here? And he knows my name. It's okay, Frankie. They're the good guys."

Frankie stilled, and while she couldn't clearly make out all his features, she could see his eyes studying hers. Then he nodded.

It was reason four hundred and sixty-seven why she loved this man. He was out of his element, but he believed her when she said they were safe. She placed the weapon she was holding on top of the crates then took Frankie's hand and stood. She held her other hand out to her side, making sure the men who'd arrived could see she was unarmed. Yes, they were on the same side and they'd been sent to rescue them, but she didn't want to do anything that might make them think they were a threat.

She assumed the men had night-vision goggles and could see her and Frankie quite clearly, so she slowly stepped out from behind the crates, Frankie at her side, and said, "We're here. Situation is under control."

"Captain Fletcher?" another man asked.

"Yes," Annie said.

"And is Franklin Sanders with you?"

"I'm here," Frankie said.

"Any injuries?"

"Only the bad guys," Annie said.

She heard someone chuckle. "That's what Tex said we'd find."

Annie smiled for the first time in what seemed like hours. She *knew* Tex would come through. He might claim that he was getting too old to constantly monitor everyone in his ever-growing circle, but she knew better.

"You wearing eyes?" Annie asked, referring to a body cam.

"Yes, Ma'am," the man in charge of the rescue said.

Annie nodded at him. "Thank you, Tex," she said fervently. She knew he'd see this video, probably before she and Frankie even got back to their ship.

"Goggles off!" someone yelled, and Annie turned to Frankie.

"Close your eyes," she told him. Without questioning her, he did as she asked. Once more, love rose up within Annie at his immediate trust. Turning into him, Annie closed her own eyes and rested her forehead against his shoulder.

Even with her eyes shut, she could easily see when their rescuers turned on their high-powered lights so they could assess the situation better. She heard Garrett begging to be released, and one of the men telling him to shut the fuck up.

Smiling, she opened her eyes and looked up at Frankie. He was staring down at her with an expression she couldn't decipher. "What?"

Frankie shook his head. "If I was reading a book and this happened, I'd probably throw the thing across the room. It's just so unbelievable."

Annie chuckled. "I know. I've got some overprotective uncles, that's for sure."

"Excuse me, Ma'am." The same soldier she'd been talking to a moment ago approached. "I need to make sure you're good," he said almost apologetically.

But she understood. He probably had strict orders to take care of any injuries she or Frankie might have sustained. Stepping back from Frankie, Annie turned to him. "I'm fine. Cuts and bruises. That's it."

"How're your ribs?" the man asked.

That clinched it—these men had definitely been sent by Tex. Annie couldn't stop the smile from crossing her face. "They're fine."

"What about you, sir? Can I take a look at that cut on your forehead?"

"I can take care of it if you get me some cleanser and bandages," Annie told him.

The man nodded. He stepped away, then turned back to her. "Not that I'm surprised, after hearing stories about your record from Tex, but good job on subduing these assholes. You shoot him?"

Annie shook her head. "No. Frankie and Garrett, the

guy who's hogtied, were fighting over his pistol and a shot went wide. Hit his own brother."

"While Annie was fighting him," Frankie muttered darkly.

The man's eyes widened and he whistled low. But he merely nodded. "That tourniquet probably saved his life."

Annie nodded. He didn't need to tell her that. "By the way, their buddies are supposed to arrive sometime in the morning to pick them up, as well as the crates of drugs."

The man's eyes lit up as if excited about the prospect of intercepting the newcomers. "Ten-four. We'll get you two out of here and we'll set up a perimeter. We'll catch them."

"And, in return for me helping his brother, Garrett promised to tell the authorities everything."

"Everything?" the man asked with a grin.

"Everything," Annie confirmed.

"Excellent. If you two want to wait over by the Zodiac, we'll get you out of here in a jiffy. You can look at your man's head in the boat."

Annie nodded. She was all for getting out of here. And getting a ride back to their ship was much preferred than trying to find their way back on the barely there trails they'd used to get to this side of the island. "We're going back to our sailboat, right?" she asked.

The man looked uncomfortable for the first time. "Um, we were instructed to take you to Nassau."

"No," Annie said firmly. "We have almost a week left on our vacation, and I'm not giving that up."

The man obviously had no idea what to say to that.

Annie forced herself to speak in a calmer tone. "We're

fine, Sergeant. You did your job and found us, safe and sound. Neither of us is wounded. We just want to finish our vacation."

He still didn't look convinced.

Annie let go of Frankie's hand and stepped closer to the man. She looked directly into the camera strapped to the middle of his chest. "Tex, I'm fine. Frankie's fine. You did exactly what I needed you to do, you sent in the cavalry. Thank you for always having my back. But we're going to our ship, where we can relax for another week. Okay?"

She heard the sergeant chuckling and glanced up at him. "You know this isn't a live feed, right?" he asked.

"That's what you think," Annie mumbled. Then louder, she said, "I just know Tex, and if he truly wants me home, he'll make it happen. I wouldn't be surprised if we got back to the ship and found all our stuff packed and waiting to be offloaded."

The soldier looked uncomfortable once again.

"Shit, let me guess, Tex gave you orders to pick up all our luggage too, didn't he?"

"Um...yes, Ma'am."

"Well, you can forget that. I haven't had a true vacation in too many years to count and I'm not cutting this one short," Annie said firmly.

"It's okay, love," Frankie said, putting his arm around her waist.

Annie realized that she'd taken another step toward the soldier and was ready to actually take him on if he disagreed.

"I'm sure Tex knows how hard you work and how

177

much you need this vacation. Especially after how stressful things have been for you lately...you know, with your teams and the incident on your last mission. He wouldn't dare take this away from you. He knows it would stress you out even more. Besides, I'm *sure* he knows that if we ran into more trouble, you'd take care of it and be just fine. You're Annie Fletcher, after all. Fletch's daughter wouldn't let some random drug dealers get the better of her."

Annie smiled up at Frankie. She knew he was talking as much to her and the soldier standing in front of them, as he was Tex, who was probably watching them right this second. Her man was manipulative, but since he was using his smarts in their favor, she was one hundred percent onboard. "You're right. Tex would know that forcing me to do anything I didn't want to do would backfire. What do you think—is sending thank you notes and presents every day for a year enough to drive him over the edge?"

Annie smirked. Everyone knew Tex hated to be thanked. It was a quirk of his.

She looked up at the soldier standing awkwardly in front of them. "Seriously, it's fine. We're good, you and your men can take care of the drug pickup and Garrett and Travis. Frankie and I will go back to our ship, and I promise to behave. We'll even stay on the ship at all the remaining ports if that makes everyone feel better."

The sergeant sighed, but nodded. "All right. If you'd just go wait by the Zodiac, we'll get you on your way soon."

Annie turned and headed for the surf before the man had even finished talking. She had no doubt that Tex had seen and heard her loud and clear. He'd tell her dad that they were fine, and that they were finishing their vacation.

Fletch would give them the third degree about what the hell happened, but for now, she was relatively sure she and Frankie would get to finish their vacation.

And she hadn't lied. She was perfectly happy to stay onboard for the duration. Annie was well aware that it was her and Frankie's fault they were in the dangerous situation they'd found themselves in. If they'd stayed on the path, they'd be asleep on the sailboat right now.

But then again, if they hadn't broken the rules, millions of dollars of drugs would soon be on the streets back home. Annie couldn't regret their actions, simply because they'd had a very small part in fighting the drug trade.

The soldier who'd been left in charge of the Zodiac helped them both onboard and Annie did her best to clean and bandage Frankie's cut.

It was probably only five minutes later when the sergeant shouted, "Lights out in thirty!"

Knowing the beach was going to be plunged into darkness once again, Annie leaned against Frankie. He put his arm around her and held her tightly against his side. She caught a glimpse of Garrett being carried across the beach, still hogtied. He was dumped unceremoniously into the bottom of the Zodiac, his brother placed a little more gently next to him. Then the sergeant and one other man got on either side of the boat just as the bright lights on the beach were turned off.

The two men easily pushed the Zodiac back into the surf and soon they were on the water, hopefully heading for their ship.

There was just enough ambient light to see as Frankie turned to her and signed, *The others aren't coming with us?*

I'm sure they're setting up a perimeter to take out whoever comes to pick up the drugs, Annie told him. *I'm guessing they'll drop us off, then take these two to Nassau before heading back to the island.*

Frankie nodded.

"That talking with your hands is so annoying," Garrett bitched as he bounced in the bottom of the Zodiac racing over the waves.

The sergeant's foot shot out and kicked Garrett in the shoulder.

"Ouch! Watch it, man!"

"Sorry, slipped," the sergeant said, winking at Frankie and Annie. Then he signed in what Annie could only describe as "pigeon sign language," *My unit has found sign language to be very helpful on missions.*

Annie shared a look with Frankie. Once upon a time, his godfather, Cooper, had lost his hearing and been medically discharged from the Navy. Then he was hired to teach Special Forces teams sign language, much like Annie taught all of her teammates. It looked like, after twenty years, it was now more of a common thing than not.

She closed her eyes and leaned back against Frankie, feeling the stress of the day and night finally threaten to overwhelm her. She'd been concerned for her own life, of course, but having Frankie with her had been both a blessing and a curse. She couldn't imagine her life without him, and for a while, things hadn't looked so good for either of them.

But everything had worked out. She was safe. Frankie was safe. They were both hungry, thirsty, and tired, but they were alive. Nothing else mattered.

CHAPTER THIRTEEN

Frankie held Annie close and felt her relax against him. He was too keyed up to even think about closing his eyes. The soldiers on the Zodiac were wearing night-vision goggles so they could see, and even though Frankie couldn't make out more than vague shapes, he didn't close his eyes.

What he and Annie had just been through was nothing compared to what she did on a regular basis, and it made him all the more grateful she was thinking about getting out of the Army. She was very good at what she did, that much was obvious after watching her in action the last few hours, but that didn't mean someone couldn't get off a lucky shot and kill her in the future.

Being a trauma doctor wouldn't be easy, it would mean long hours and a lot of stress, but Frankie much preferred that over his Annie being shot at regularly in some of the most dangerous places in the world.

And he had no doubt she would be an amazing doctor if that was what she chose. He'd seen her with Travis, how calm she'd been and how easily she'd stopped his bleeding.

His woman would excel at whatever she chose to do, but being a doctor would benefit so many people. She'd continue to make a difference in the world.

Frankie had been lost in his thoughts, so when he saw lights ahead in the distance, for a moment, he thought he was seeing things. Then he realized they were headed right for their sailboat. There was no mistaking it, as it seemed as if every light on the vessel was ablaze, even though it was—he looked at his watch—one-thirty in the morning.

He hadn't been convinced the sergeant would agree to take them back to their ship. He knew Tex. Knew how persuasive the man could be. But if Annie wanted to finish their vacation, Frankie would do anything to make that happen. If he was being honest, he could use some alone time with her as well. After what happened, he just needed to be near her, without sharing her with family and friends. It was selfish of him, but Frankie didn't care.

The Zodiac came up alongside the ship, and Manuel was at the bottom of the stairs off the side of the vessel, waiting for them.

Thank God, you're all right, Manuel signed before he grabbed the rope at the front of the Zodiac. He lashed it to the small platform attached to the stairs and held out his hand.

Annie was alert now, but Frankie could see she was nearing her limit. She'd been in charge for hours and he was more than happy to give her a break. Frankie held her hand tightly and helped her stand. She shuffled to the side of the Zodiac and reached for Manuel. Frankie didn't let go until he was sure the other man had a firm grip on her.

She headed up the stairs, but paused four steps up and looked back, waiting for him.

"Thank you," Frankie told the sergeant, holding out his hand.

The other man shook it firmly. "Thank *you*. My sister died of a drug overdose. Any day we can stop more drugs from entering the country is a good day."

Frankie nodded at him, then turned to Manuel. He took the sailor's hand and even before he'd climbed the stairs to stand next to Annie, the Zodiac had pulled away from the ship and was heading back into the dark night.

He followed Annie as they climbed the stairs to reach the promenade deck. The captain was waiting.

"I'm so glad to see you two," he said, the relief easy to hear in his voice.

"I'm sorry for all the trouble we put you through," Annie said.

"We shouldn't have broken the rules and taken the off-limits path," Frankie added.

The captain merely shrugged. "Honestly, you aren't the first to do so. We keep telling our bosses that someone needs to come out and make a new path that doesn't have as many temptations. This island is beautiful; who wouldn't want to explore?"

Frankie knew the captain was being very gracious. He had every right to be pissed. The search for them had disrupted the ship's schedule and he'd very likely had to deal with some irate passengers. People were generally selfish, and wanted what they wanted. It didn't matter that someone was missing; if they didn't get to their next port on time, it was an irritation.

"What do you need? Food? Something to drink?"

Annie glanced back at Frankie before saying, "I could eat." Her stomach chose that moment to growl. Loudly.

They all chuckled.

"But I don't want to put anyone out," Annie added.

"It's no problem. Our baker is up now making pastries for breakfast. And if you don't mind leftovers, I'm sure we can find something for you. We usually turn the chicken and seafood that doesn't get eaten at dinner into lunch dishes. Come on, we'll go raid the kitchen."

Annie looked back at Frankie. *He's being really nice. I keep waiting for the next shoe to fall. For him to start screaming at us.*

Frankie nodded. *I think he's probably just relieved he didn't lose us. That would look bad on his record.*

True.

They followed the captain to the galley kitchen. It was small, running the width of the ship right behind the dining room. Annie and Frankie were introduced to the baker, who handed them both a slice of cinnamon-raisin bread she'd just taken out of the oven.

Frankie took a bite and closed his eyes in enjoyment.

"Holy crap, I think this is the best thing I've ever eaten," Annie said with enthusiasm.

The baker smiled. "Here, try this. It's a raspberry-apple danish."

And so it went. The baker giving them bites of the things she was cooking for breakfast, while the captain managed to unearth leftovers from the fridge that were going to be made into a salads for lunch the following day.

Frankie and Annie stuffed themselves while standing in the small galley kitchen, chatting with the captain.

When they'd finally taken the edge off their hunger, and had both drank two full glasses of water, Annie smiled at the captain. "Thank you for not waiting to report us missing."

He blinked. "Why would I wait?"

"I don't know. Because you hoped we'd come walking out of the jungle at any moment? Because you didn't want to get in trouble with your bosses? Because it would look bad?"

The captain shook his head. "When we didn't find you right away, I didn't hesitate to call for help. It can sometimes take up to a day to get someone from Nassau out here. I hoped that we'd find you in the meantime, but I didn't want to delay the assistance. I was still surprised when help came so soon though."

Frankie couldn't keep the chuckle from escaping. "The guys who came to help us weren't search-and-rescue from Nassau," he informed the captain. He was exhausted, and so damn relieved he and Annie were standing here, stuffing their faces with delicious food and not sinking into the depths of the ocean after being shot by Garrett and Travis. He probably wouldn't have said anything if he wasn't so tired.

"They weren't?"

"No."

"Who were they?"

Annie shared a look with Frankie, and he nodded. He'd already said too much, probably. He'd leave the details for Annie to disclose.

"My uncle was a SEAL. He knows people. The second our names were entered into a computer somewhere as

185

being missing, he was notified. He sent our rescuers," Annie explained.

It was a very simplified explanation, but it was enough.

"So again, thank you for not delaying asking for help," Frankie finished.

"Wow." The captain tilted his head and examined Frankie and Annie for a long moment. "I have a feeling you aren't quite what you appear."

"We're exactly who you see," Annie countered. "Two people badly in need of a vacation and madly in love."

"Uh-huh," the captain said skeptically. "On that note, I'm gonna leave you to finish up here and get some sleep."

"Did we mess up the schedule too badly?" Annie asked.

"Surprisingly, no. We were going to try to sail tomorrow morning before heading into our next port, but I've already told my relief captain to speed toward the port. We won't take the time to sail, and we'll be an hour or so late, but we'll still make it."

"Good," Annie said. She looked up at Frankie, then back at the captain. "I know we have no right to ask for any favors, not after the trouble we've caused—"

"You helped take down two drug dealers and kept a bunch of drugs from entering the US, I'd say the 'trouble' you caused was well worth it," the captain replied.

"Again, thank you for being so gracious," Annie said. "Anyway, since you're a captain of a sea vessel...can you marry us?"

Frankie blinked in surprise. "Annie," he whispered.

"That is...if you want," she said, studying Frankie.

"Of course I want that. I've always wanted it. But what

about your mom and the big wedding I'm sure she's planning right this second?"

"We can still have it. I've been an idiot, Frankie. What happened today just made that all the more clear. There's nothing I want more than to be yours. I don't want to wait one more day."

"You *are* mine," Frankie said firmly. "We don't need a piece of paper and a ring to make it true."

"If I can interrupt a second," the captain said.

Frankie and Annie both looked at him.

"It's a fallacy that all captains have the ability to marry people. But in my case, I actually *do* have the authority. The cruise company paid to register the ship in the Bahamas just so we could perform marriage ceremonies onboard and make them legally binding. However, there's paperwork and such that's required. You can't just up and decide to get hitched...there's a waiting period and all that."

Annie's shoulders sagged. "Right. Of course. It's okay."

"Let's do it anyway," Frankie said. "It might not be legal, but in our hearts, it will be."

Annie's eyes sparkled. "Really?"

"Really. You think I can deny you anything?" Frankie asked with a laugh.

"I'm sure I can get a cake made in no time," the baker said.

Frankie had forgotten she was still in the room with them.

"And we could probably get some decorations put up and have it on the back deck before lunch. Maybe not tomorrow, but the day after," the captain suggested.

"Can you marry us right now?" Annie asked.

"Now?" the captain asked.

"Yeah."

"But everyone's asleep."

"We don't need an audience. We just need the two of us," Frankie said, completely on board with what Annie was thinking.

"Oh, well...yeah, I could do that," the captain said.

"We don't want to make more work for anyone," Annie said. "Something nice and quiet will be perfect."

"You want to shower and change first?" the captain asked.

Annie looked down at herself and laughed. "Frankie?" she asked.

He shook his head. "No. I think now is perfect."

"All right then. Where should we do this?" the captain asked, smiling.

"Up front by the bridge," Annie said, as if she'd spent time thinking about it.

"It'll be windy," the captain warned.

"Doesn't matter," Annie assured him.

Five minutes later, Frankie stood face-to-face with Annie on the deck next to the bridge. The wind was blowing hard, just as the captain promised, since they were motoring fast to make their next port. It was three o'clock in the morning, they were both tired, smelled like sweat, still had sand sticking to their bodies—and both of them were smiling so wide, it wasn't hard to see how happy they were.

Frankie had never seen anyone as beautiful as his Annie was at that moment. He also wasn't surprised she'd managed to talk the captain into this. She was the kind of person others seemed to bend over backward to please.

"Ready?" the captain asked.

"Ready," Frankie and Annie said in unison.

"I'm gonna keep this short and sweet," he said. "I'm honored today to be officiating and witnessing the joining of Annie and Frankie. Life is a series of twists and turns, and finding someone to take the ride with you isn't easy. But when you know, you know, and it's obvious that the two of you are meant to be together. Frankie, do you take Annie to be your lawfully wedded wife? To have and hold, honor and cherish, in sickness and health, for as long as you both shall live?"

"I do," Frankie said.

"Annie, do you take Frankie to be your lawfully wedded husband? To have and hold, honor and cherish, in sickness and health, for as long as you both shall live?"

"I do," Annie said.

"Do you want to exchange personal vows?" the captain asked.

Annie looked up at Frankie, obviously letting him make the decision.

"Yes," he blurted. Not at all sure what he was going to say. For a moment, he panicked, wondering how he could possibly find the words to make this amazing woman understand just how much he loved her.

Then they poured out of him through his fingers. He signed his vows since his throat seemed to be closed, and he knew he'd flub them up if he tried to speak.

Annie, I knew from the second I saw you that I wanted you to be mine forever. Someway, somehow, I was determined to one day make you my wife. You're my best friend, my biggest supporter, my lover. I promise to give you all my words, both spoken and signed, when needed, and to stay silent when they aren't. I will support you unconditionally in whatever you want to do. Be that a doctor or the best damn circus clown there's ever been. I will be the best man I can be for you, and if the time comes, the best dad for our children. I'm overwhelmed with love and gratitude to be standing here in front of you. I'm proud, and lucky as hell, and I know it. I love you, Ann Elizabeth Grant Fletcher, soon to be Sanders.

Annie followed Frankie's lead and signed her own vows.

You were mine from the moment we met, Frankie. There's never been anyone else for me. And there never will be. You were my reason for trying to be the best person I could be back then, just as you are now. You strengthen my weaknesses and bring focus to my dreams. Together, we're the perfect team, we always have been. You will never come second in my life. Ever. You are always on my mind no matter where I am or what I'm doing.

"I love you," Frankie blurted when she was done.

"And I love you," Annie echoed.

Frankie took her face in his hands and bent forward. Her hair blew between them and he got a mouthful of the strands when he kissed her, but it didn't matter. Nothing mattered but the woman in his arms being healthy and whole.

They were both laughing when he pulled back and Frankie tried to smooth her hair behind her ears...with no luck.

"I guess that's my cue to say, I now pronounce you man and wife," the captain said. "Congratulations."

As Frankie stared down at Annie, he knew this was what he could expect from the rest of their life. Laughter, love, and definitely the unconventional. They'd beaten the odds from the moment they met. Who would've thought an outgoing little girl like Annie would take a liking to him, a shy deaf boy who she couldn't even talk to? But she had, and Frankie had known even back then that Annie was his future. That he would do whatever it took to make her happy.

Because when Annie was happy, *he* was happy.

"I'm guessing we won't see you at breakfast," the captain said with a grin.

"You'd guess right," Frankie told him.

"And to put your mind at ease, we're not planning on getting off at any of the ports either," Annie said. "I kind of promised my family we'd be good and stay put until we arrived back in Barbados."

"You told them?" the captain asked. "When?"

"It's a long story. I didn't talk directly to my dad or anything," Annie said with a smile as she stared up at Frankie.

"No problem. You aren't required to go to shore. If you need anything, just let me or one of my staff know. We really are relieved you're all right."

"Thanks, we are too," Frankie said.

"Happy wedding day," the captain said, smiling at them both before heading down the deck toward the stairs, and most likely his bed.

Instead of leading her to their own room, Frankie took Annie in his arms, and she stared at him in confusion. "What are you doing?"

"Dancing with my wife," Frankie said. "First dance and all that."

Annie smiled and snuggled into him, resting her head on his shoulder. There was more shuffling back and forth than actual dancing, but Frankie didn't care. How long they stood out in the wind and darkness, he didn't know, too focused on the woman in his arms.

He knew it was time to take Annie to their room when she jerked suddenly, as if she'd fallen asleep standing up. "Come on." He chuckled, wrapping an arm around her waist. "I don't know about you, but I'm ready to sleep for twelve hours straight."

"Me too," Annie said, then yawned huge.

Frankie wished he had the energy to make love to his wife, but there would be time for that later. She needed to shower, then sleep. Since there wasn't room in their miniscule bathroom for both of them to shower at the same time, he'd gladly let her go first. She'd be dead to the world by the time he was cleaned up, but that was fine. She'd more than earned her rest.

Twenty minutes later, Frankie snuggled up behind his wife.

His *wife*.

The ceremony might not have been legal in the court's eyes, but this would always be the date he celebrated their anniversary. Annie had been worth the twenty-year wait. Hell, he would've waited twenty more. He didn't need a piece of paper to know Annie was his and he was hers. They were connected body, mind, and soul.

And tomorrow, when everyone else was on shore shopping and eating and doing whatever activity the cruise line had planned for them, he'd physically show his wife how much she meant to him.

Frankie fell asleep with a huge grin on his face. Today had been another adventure in the amazing life he knew he'd have with his Annie. Hopefully future escapades wouldn't include guns and drugs, but if they did, his kickass Green Beret would keep them safe.

CHAPTER FOURTEEN

Six days later, on their last night on the ship, Annie lay in bed with Frankie and sighed with contentment. They'd kept their promise and hadn't stepped foot off the ship since their rescue. Just about all of the guests—including Megan, Dottie, Joseph, and Bill—had been extremely understanding about what had happened. No one was upset that the journey had been delayed and everyone seemed relieved they were all right.

Annie wasn't sure if their dinner dates from that first night were lying, but ultimately it didn't matter. All that mattered was that they were safe.

"What are you thinking, Mrs. Sanders?" Frankie asked.

Annie grinned. She'd never get tired of hearing that. Intellectually, she knew they weren't legally married, they hadn't done any paperwork and wouldn't bother, but that night a week ago would always feel like their official anniversary. "This has been nice," she said. "I've traveled a lot, thanks to the Army, but I've never been able to relax like this while doing it."

Frankie tightened his arm around her. Annie was on her side, her head resting on his shoulder, her fingers gently tracing circles on his bare chest. They'd made love earlier, and she was basking in the easy intimacy they shared afterward. Tomorrow would be busy, they'd be back in Barbados and had a plane to catch, but for now, it felt as if it was just her and Frankie alone in the world.

"If we were here much longer, you'd go crazy, admit it," Frankie said with a small laugh.

Annie grinned. He was right. She'd never been one to enjoy lazing around too often. Even as a child she was constantly on the go, according to her mom. "True," she said after a moment. "Does it bother you?" she asked.

"No," Frankie said without hesitation. "I love you exactly how you are. We balance each other out."

Annie nodded. They did. They'd always been that way. Annie was the outgoing one who loved to take chances. Frankie was reserved, preferring to hang back and get the lay of the land before acting. Knowing he had her back was one of the reasons why Annie felt so confident in trying new things. If it didn't work out, Frankie would be there to catch her when she fell.

Propping her head on her hand, Annie studied the man she'd loved practically her entire life.

"What?" Frankie eventually asked when she didn't say anything.

"I feel as if I've underestimated you," Annie blurted.

He frowned. "No, you haven't."

"I have," Annie insisted. She'd thought about this a lot in the last week. "When we were out there, we worked together perfectly. I've never clicked with anyone out in the field quite like we did."

"It was you," Frankie said modestly. "You're one of the best leaders I've ever seen. You make it easy to follow."

"No," Annie insisted. "You're not giving yourself enough credit. They didn't even tie you up, Frankie. They were so sure you weren't a threat, you played your part so well. But when you charged Travis, then Garrett...I've never been so scared in my life."

"I would've done anything to keep them from touching you. From hurting you," Frankie said firmly.

"I know. That's what I'm talking about," Annie said. "All my life, people have told me how amazing I am. How strong. How smart. How funny. I excelled in ROTC at college and had no doubt I'd make the Green Berets. In all the time I've known you, you've always been my quiet supporter. Never wanting to be in the spotlight, never wanting any accolades. And this week has opened my eyes and made me see that I've accomplished what I have in the Army *because* of you. Because of your support. Because you've encouraged me and never even blinked when I came home and said we were moving. Again. Every time I got called up for a mission, you reassured me that things at home would be fine, told me not to worry about you, and to go out there and do my job."

Annie's eyes filled with tears. "I've taken advantage of you, and I hate that. I've been selfish and too focused on myself and what I want. You're incredible, Frankie. It's because of *you* that I have the courage to be brave. And I need you a hell of a lot more than you'll ever need me."

"Wrong," Frankie said, rolling until Annie was staring

up at him from her back. "You haven't taken advantage of me at all, because everything I've done has been because I love you. If you said you wanted to live in the desert of Africa, I'd agree in a heartbeat. I'd follow you anywhere. You mean that much to me. You believed in me every time it felt like no one else did. You supported me unconditionally. When I had my implant surgery, your voice was the first one I wanted to hear above all others. I love you, Annie. I was completely out of my element out there, and was only following your lead."

Annie closed her eyes and felt Frankie brush his thumb gently beneath, wiping away her tears. After a minute to gather herself, she opened them to his loving expression.

"I'm going to talk to my commander when I get back to post. I want out."

Frankie's forehead furrowed. "Are you sure? You don't have to decide anything right this second."

"I know," Annie told him. "And I'm sure. What happened on that island made the decision easy. I've been worrying about what everyone *else* would think about my decision, when really the only opinions that matter are yours and mine. No one else is living my life. No one else is on the front lines tracking down terrorists and seeing the worst of humanity. Just me. No one else is saying goodbye to the love of their life and hoping they'll see them again when the mission is over. Just you. Yes, I want my dad and everyone else to be proud of me, but it's finally hit home that they already are. I don't have to prove anything to anyone.

"And when we were out there, and I realized that I could lose you—all it would've taken was one of those assholes getting spooked—I understood exactly what you must go through every time I get deployed. I don't want that for you, Frankie, and I don't want it for me."

"Don't quit because of me," Frankie said sternly.

"I'm not," Annie said without hesitation. "I'm doing it *for* you. And for me. I can serve my country by being a doctor. By saving lives in a hospital. I'm proud of what I've done in the Army. Proud of being one of the first women to become a Green Beret. I'd like to think I've paved the way for other women to do the same thing. But I can be proud of myself for being a doctor too. I can save lives instead of taking them, without putting my own on the line."

"Yes, you can," Frankie said. "And your dad and everyone else will be just as proud of you for that as they are now."

"I hope so, but if they're disappointed that I'm getting out...I can't help that. I have to do what's right for me and you. They aren't living our lives, we are."

Frankie smiled, and Annie could see the relief behind his eyes. Her man never would've come right out and said he wanted her to quit, but she could tell that he wasn't upset in the least with her decision. "It's not going to be easy," she warned.

Frankie laughed. "*Life* isn't easy," he countered. "But no matter how tough it gets, we'll face it together."

"Like we did on that island."

"Exactly."

They smiled at each other for a beat, then Frankie said, "Wherever you go, whatever you do, I'll be there. I'm not ashamed or afraid to stand behind you, Annie. People can think what they want about our relationship, and if they think I'm pussy-whipped, I don't give a shit. Because I am. I'll gladly let you have the limelight but I'll always be there to protect you, no matter what that means."

That felt good. Really good.

"And I'll protect you too," she told him.

"No one fucks with us," Frankie said with a smile.

"Nope. And we have the advantage of being able to speak without words," Annie added.

"That *is* helpful," Frankie said. "Like when you're a famous doctor and we have to attend fundraisers and I can't stand how beautiful you are in your dress, I can tell you from across the room that I want to take you home and fuck you until you can't walk."

Annie grinned. "I hate wearing dresses," she reminded him.

"I know. Which makes it even more special when you do," Frankie said.

It was just another reason why she loved her man. He let her be exactly who she was, and never let her apologize for it.

"Our people are gonna be insane when we get home," Annie warned.

"I know."

And Annie figured he did. Not only would Fletch lose his mind about what had almost happened, all his friends would too. Her mom would be extra clingy, wanting to talk on the phone every night until she got it through her head that her baby was okay. And that was *before* any wedding planning happened.

"Our lives are going to be crazy for the next year or so,"

she added. "As I transition out of the Army and we figure out our new normal."

"Yup," Frankie said easily.

Annie sighed and decided they'd talked enough. It was almost impossible to get Frankie worked up. He took things as they came and was her rock when she got overly stressed. Now that she'd finally made a decision, she needed to talk to her commander about chaptering out of the Army, apply for med schools, move, plan a wedding. Just thinking about the chaos she was about to experience was enough to drive her blood pressure up. But right now, she wanted to enjoy this last night with her husband.

"What is that grin for?" Frankie asked.

"My husband," Annie said simply.

"My wife," he replied.

Then Annie pushed on Frankie's chest until he rolled again. She straddled his waist and smiled. His eyes were glued to her chest. She couldn't help arching her back slightly, pushing her breasts out. His hands came up and palmed her tits, playing with her nipples as her breathing increased.

Knowing he could easily distract her from her plans, Annie forced herself to scoot backward, until his hands dropped to his sides. He spread his legs, giving her room to kneel between them.

Just when she thought he was going to let her take charge, one hand shot into her hair, grabbing a handful and holding her tightly.

"Don't make me come," he ordered.

Annie pouted at him.

"I mean it. I want to be inside you when I lose it."

She felt him loosen his grip enough for her to nod, then he gave her the sexiest grin before pushing her head toward his lap.

Annie went gladly. She loved this man more than she had the words to tell him. So she'd just have to show him instead.

Frankie was sorry to see the ship they'd spent the last two weeks on fading into the sun. It would always have a soft spot in his heart, even after what had almost happened to him and Annie. He hated that she'd come so close to being hurt, but he was as proud of her as he could be. He'd always known what a good soldier she was, but he never thought he'd get to see it firsthand.

He'd also spent some of the best nights of his life in bed with his wife on that ship. Their room was small with no frills, but for him, it might as well have been a suite in a castle. His love was there; he couldn't have asked for anything else.

That morning at breakfast, they'd exchanged emails with a few people and said their goodbyes. Frankie and Annie had spent some time with Manuel, promising to stay in touch. He'd become much more confident in his signing over the last two weeks and was grateful for the opportunity to practice.

The captain had surprised them both with a signed certificate of marriage. He'd warned that it wasn't legal, as it didn't have the stamp or signatures of the Bahamian authorities, but neither Frankie nor Annie cared. It was a welcome gift, and one they'd cherish forever.

He'd also told them he'd gotten word from the authorities that the drug runners who'd arrived to pick up the crates had been intercepted and were now in jail back in Nassau. Not only that, but apparently Garrett hadn't gone back on his word, telling them everything he knew about the operation. It was a small victory, though Frankie knew someone would take their place in the cog of the drug trade.

Travis was still in the hospital but expected to make a full recovery...after which, he'd be transferred to jail alongside his brother.

Annie squeezed Frankie's hand and he glanced at her. The bus was hot and crowded, and smelled a little funky, but neither cared.

"Love you," Annie said.

"Not as much as I love you," Frankie retorted.

She rolled her eyes at him.

Their flight wasn't supposed to leave until later that afternoon, and as a part of the package, they were given a tour of the island before they headed to the airport. The only surprise of the day was when they checked in for their flight and found they'd been upgraded to first class.

"Tex?" Frankie asked Annie as they stood in line for security.

"That would be my guess," she said, on the same wavelength as usual. "Either him or the cruise line decided to upgrade us."

"After we caused them so much trouble?" Frankie asked with a quirk of an eyebrow.

Annie chuckled. "Right. Probably not. Most definitely Tex."

Some men would be uncomfortable with the former SEAL's power and the way he seemed to always know what was going on with him and his woman. But not Frankie. Tex had given Annie her first pair of earrings, which had trackers in them. She'd stopped wearing them when she was a teenager, not comfortable with her dad's friend knowing where she was all the time, but she did put them in whenever she was deployed. She was cautious, not stupid.

Annie wasn't lying when she said things would be insane when they got home. Mostly because of how they'd need to reassure all of her dad's friends that they were okay. Even though Annie was a Special Forces soldier, to them, she'd always be the little girl they doted on as she grew up.

She also needed to sit down with her mom and dad and let them know she'd made her decision about the Army and her future. She still wanted their support, but Frankie was relieved to know she wasn't nearly as stressed about their reactions as she was before. She was doing what was best for her and their future. That was what mattered most.

They found two seats next to each other in the airport, and despite having two and a half hours to wait before their flight, Annie seemed content to sit next to him and people watch.

"You okay?" Frankie asked her.

"Yeah, why?"

"You usually don't like to sit," he said with a shrug.

"You walk around, window shop, get some water...you know. You fidget."

Annie smiled and reached for his hand. "I know. But today I think I just want to sit here next to you and appreciate life for a bit."

"I'm okay with that," Frankie said, lifting their clasped hands and kissing her fingers. "But if you get itchy feet, feel free to roam. I'll watch our stuff."

"I know you will," Annie said. "You're too good to me."

"No such thing," Frankie told her.

Annie's ability to sit still and appreciate life lasted about forty minutes—thirty more than Frankie thought she'd make it. She gave him a sheepish grin and said she was going to take a walk. Frankie kissed her cheek and told her to be careful. He watched as she strolled down the concourse, noting the admiring glances men gave her when she passed. He wasn't worried about her flirting back. As long as he'd known her, she'd never shown interest in anyone else.

For what seemed like the millionth time, he thanked his lucky stars that Annie had chosen him. He vowed to be the best man he could be for her. She deserved the world, and even though he could only give her his own small part of it, he could fill it with enough love, laughter, and happiness to last a lifetime.

CHAPTER FIFTEEN

Annie laughed as her dad scowled at the low-crawl obstacle on the Army post.

"I don't remember the damn thing being so close to the ground," Fletch muttered as he walked around it. "If I get down there, I'll never be able to get back up."

Annie laughed harder. Damn, she loved her dad. She had no doubt that Fletch could get down on his belly in the dirt and spring back up when he got through the obstacle, but he was probably more worried about her mom scolding him for getting his shirt dirty when he got home.

Ten months had passed since she and Frankie had gotten home from their Caribbean trip. And they'd been going nonstop every single day. Fletch wasn't surprised by her decision to get out of the Army. He admitted that while he had the utmost respect for her skills, he was relieved he wouldn't have to worry about her while she was deployed anymore.

She'd informed her commander that she was chaptering out, had been rejected by three schools, and was happy to be accepted to the University of Texas at Austin. It was her first choice, even if it wasn't the best school in Texas. Annie liked the thought of being close to her family for the first time in a decade. Her parents weren't getting any younger, although they still looked very good for their age.

She liked that she'd get to spend more time with John as he finished high school, as well as all her cousins. Frankie's dad had decided to retire to Texas himself, but that decision was more because a woman he'd met online lived in San Antonio. Frankie had been overjoyed that he'd get to see his father more often as well.

Now that med school had started, and Annie was as busy as ever studying her ass off.

She and Frankie were both relieved the move would hopefully be their last for a long while. She felt guilty that he was once more taking on the bulk of the responsibilities at home. Cleaning, cooking, shopping, and dealing with the hundred little things that came up when setting up a new house. But he constantly reassured her that he didn't mind, was happy to do his part to make her life easier.

Her mom had done most of the planning of their wedding, and Annie felt bad about that too for a while, but her mom promised she was having the time of her life, so she just let her go with it.

Tomorrow, Annie would officially become Frankie's wife. While they both still considered their Caribbean wedding their true anniversary date, it would be a relief to finally be able to call him her husband legally.

She'd said goodbye to Frankie earlier that evening, when he'd gone with his dad and godfather to a hotel. He wasn't thrilled about it but didn't raise a stink. Annie wasn't too excited about it either; she hated spending the night away from her man. She'd become addicted to sleeping next to him every night, now that she wasn't deployed every other month.

Around eight-thirty, Fletch had asked if she wanted to go to post and run the obstacle course with him one more time as his little girl. Annie didn't hesitate to agree... although she told him that she'd always be his little girl.

She watched as Fletch easily ran through the course. He'd always been larger than life in her eyes, and the ease with which he pulled himself up and over barriers, despite his bitching, just made her laugh again. She followed behind him, letting her dad win for old times' sake. When they'd gone through the course twice, Fletch motioned to a bench with his head.

Annie had a feeling this was coming. Of *course* her dad didn't really want to work out so late the night before her wedding. He wanted to talk to her. She sat next to Fletch and absently noticed that he wasn't even breathing hard. She hoped she was in half as good a shape as he was when she was his age.

"So, tomorrow's the day," Fletch said.

Annie smiled. "Yeah."

"Life's funny," her dad mused.

Annie waited for him to continue, but when he didn't, she said, "It is."

Fletch sighed. "I'm not ready," he admitted.

"Dad," Annie said gently.

"I know, I know. You're twenty-eight years old. An adult. Self-sufficient and haven't lived at home in a decade. But you'll always be my little sprite. I remember when I first met your mom...she asked me if I minded if you asked questions. I was confused. I mean, of course I didn't mind. But she said I didn't understand. That you were a *really* curious child, and asked a *lot* of questions. I wasn't ready for you then, either," Fletch admitted. "But that first day you peered around the corner of the garage while I was working on an engine, I was a goner. You were covered in dirt, and you *did* ask me a million questions. You said my name was funny and scrunched up your face when I said something you didn't understand."

Annie felt tears in her eyes, but didn't interrupt.

"And you slayed me when you came to me for help when your mom was sick and you were hungry. I knew from that day forward, I'd do whatever it took to make sure you always had whatever you needed to grow up and become the amazing woman I was certain you'd be some-day. And you more than exceeded all my expectations, sprite."

Annie was crying now. "Dad," she sighed.

Fletch didn't look at her, stared straight ahead and kept talking, as if he needed to get the words out or he wouldn't be able to say them at all. "I wasn't sure about Frankie at first. I mean, he was a nice enough kid, but he lived in California. I figured you'd get bored when you didn't see him all the time. But I underestimated you, just as I think many people do when they first meet you. You were so happy for him when he got his cochlear implant. He was over-the-moon proud of you when you won that debate competition in the eighth grade. I watched the two of you grow up and fall more and more in love. But it wasn't until you got hurt your junior year, and Frankie got on a bus and came all the way out here to see for himself that you were all right, that I understood I'd lose you to him one day."

"You aren't losing me," Annie argued.

Fletch turned and looked at Annie then, and she was stunned to see tears in his eyes.

Fletch didn't cry. Ever.

"I love you, sprite. I'm proud of you. You're my only daughter and my baby. I have so many amazing memories of you, including tooling around in that damn tank, terrorizing the neighborhood."

Annie smiled through her tears.

"Frankie's a good man. He's always been your biggest supporter, and I know he'll protect you with his life, if it comes to that. A father couldn't ask for more for his daughter. You did good. Really good."

Annie couldn't stand it anymore. She threw herself at Fletch and buried her face in his chest. As his arms closed around her, she couldn't help but feel as if she was seven years old again. Fletch had always represented safety. He'd always been there when she needed him. "I love you, Dad."

"Same, sprite. Same."

They sat together on the bench for a while until they both had their emotions under control.

"One more pass for old times' sake?" Fletch asked.

"You think you can do it and not be sore as shit tomorrow?" Annie asked. "I wouldn't want you hobbling around at my wedding."

"As if," Fletch scoffed. "I can still run circles around you."

"Wanna bet?"

"No."

Annie burst out laughing. "Come on, Dad," she said, standing and holding out her hand. "We'll do it together like we used to."

"Except back then I helped *you*," Fletch grumbled.

Annie rolled her eyes. "Give me a break. You don't need help, Dad. You're still a badass Delta. You've got this."

"Damn straight I do," Fletch said.

Then he and Annie walked hand-in-hand to the start of the obstacle course.

"Ready?" Annie asked.

When her dad nodded, she counted down. "Three, Two, One, Go!"

Emily shook her head at Fletch as he hobbled out of the bathroom toward their bed.

"You just *had* to overdo it the night before your daughter's wedding, didn't you?" she asked.

"She started it," Fletch mumbled.

Emily laughed and snuggled up to her husband after he crawled under the covers. It was late and they had to be up very early tomorrow. She'd planned for manicures and pedicures for everyone. Then hair and makeup appointments. The photographer would be coming by the church to take pre-wedding pictures. The day would be full from the moment they woke up until late in the night, whenever the reception finally ended. It would be an exhausting and exciting day...and Emily couldn't help but feel just a little sad about it all.

"You have a good talk?" she asked her husband.

Fletch sighed and rested his head on top of Emily's. "I still can't believe she's getting married tomorrow."

"We knew this day would come."

"I know."

"I'm still a little amazed that she and Frankie made it," Emily mused. "They had so much going against them."

"When you know, you know," Fletch said.

"True," Emily replied, thinking back to when she and Fletch first met. "Although sometimes life puts obstacles in the way."

"That was me being an ass," Fletch said without hesitation.

Emily shook her head. "No, it was us not communicating like adults. I was too worried about taking care of Annie, and you were—"

"Too busy being jealous," Fletch said, finishing her sentence.

"That's not what I was going to say," Emily protested.

"But it's true. I'm a lucky son-of-a-bitch and I know it. You put up with a lot, with me being in the Army and being deployed as much as I was. Hell, you were kidnapped because of me."

"Not your fault, Fletch," Emily soothed. She hated that he still thought about the incident with Jacks. It had been so long ago.

"It was, but fine. I know you don't like to talk about it. Then you survived our house being blown up."

"And you've given me three amazing sons. And you've spoiled us all rotten. Our lives haven't always been sunshine and roses, but I haven't ever doubted that if I've needed you, you'd be there."

"I'll always be there for you, Em. No matter what. I love you. You're the best thing that's ever happened to me."

"And you're the best thing that's ever happened to *me*," she replied. "We aren't going to have a second to breathe tomorrow, and we need to get some sleep...but first, I'm thinking my husband needs some TLC."

"I do, huh?" Fletch asked with a smirk.

"Yup. And because I'm a good wife, and I know how sore you probably are from going overboard to try to prove to our daughter that you're in the same shape you were twenty years ago, I'll do all the work. You just have to lie there."

"Ooh, I like the sound of that," Fletch growled as he rolled onto his back and put his hands behind his head.

Emily knew full well her husband wouldn't ever just "lie there" as they made love. But she enjoyed their teasing. She straddled him and eased her nightshirt over her head. Fletch's eyes dilated. Emily wasn't as young as she used to be, and she sagged in more places than she liked, but the look of lust in her husband's eyes, even after all this time, never failed to make her feel like the sexiest woman in the world.

Fletch's hands came up to hold her hips. "Good thing I forgot to put on underwear after my shower, isn't it?"

Emily rolled her eyes.

He grinned for a moment, then sobered. "I love you, Emily."

"I love you too." Then she showed him exactly how much.

Annie stood in a back room of the same church where her mom had gotten married all those years ago, taking in everyone around her.

Rayne was helping Mary with her hair, Harley was talking with Kassie in the corner, Casey was trying to entertain her nine-year-old daughter so she didn't wrinkle her dress, Sadie was messing with her mascara, and Wendy was sitting with Akilah in the corner, having what looked like an intense conversation.

The day had been busy, but everything was going off without a hitch. Her mom had planned things carefully. The wedding coordinator had been running here and there all morning and afternoon, but as far as Annie was concerned, everything was perfect.

Annie's mom stopped next to her. "Do you think we can have a moment?" she asked softly.

Annie took a deep breath. "My mascara is waterproof, but I'm sure the makeup artist is gonna be pissed if she has to start over," she half-joked.

Emily just smiled.

She couldn't tell her mom no. "Come on," she said, reaching for her hand and pulling her toward the door. "We'll be back!" Annie yelled to the room. "Nobody freak.

Nobody leave. I'm marrying Frankie at four o'clock sharp. If you miss it, you miss it!"

Everyone laughed as she left the room with Emily. They walked down the hall and into a smaller room nearby. It was where Annie had gotten dressed earlier. It was really more of a large closet than an actual room, but it had a small window and was currently unoccupied.

When they were alone, Emily smiled at her daughter. "You look beautiful."

Annie *felt* beautiful. She wasn't a fan of girly-girl dresses and everyone knew it. When she'd seen this dress, she'd known she had to have it. It didn't have one speck of lace anywhere. It hugged her upper body and flared out at her hips. It had little cap sleeves and, best of all, it was a dark emerald green.

Annie had worried that Frankie would think it was weird that her dress wasn't white, but when she'd told him, he'd merely shrugged and said she could wear any-damn-thing she wanted, as long as she said "I do" when the time came.

She felt like a fairy princess in the dress. Her hair was pulled away from her face, but left hanging down her back. It wasn't as long as it used to be in her teens—shorter hair was easier on missions—but she was looking forward to growing it back out.

Annie held out a foot and pulled up the hem of her dress, showing off her shoes. "I love the shoes Dad found for me."

"He scoured the Internet for those," Emily said with a smile. "And when he couldn't find any combat boots with sparkles on them, he paid an obnoxious amount of money to a lady on Etsy to make them for you."

"They're perfect," Annie said. Then she looked at her mom. She didn't remember a lot of her early childhood, just bits and pieces here and there. But she *did* recall her mom always being there. She'd heard the story about how Emily had been sick from hunger, too poor to feed them both, and how Annie had gone to Fletch's house for help. While she didn't remember all the details herself, Annie *did* recall how worried she'd been about her mom. She was larger than life back then, and when she hadn't moved from the couch in over a day, Annie knew Fletch would save her. Save them both.

Emily was Annie's best friend. Had been her entire life. And now that Annie had experienced life as a soldier first-hand, she had a new appreciation for how strong her mom was as well.

"I have a present for you," Emily said, reaching into the pocket of her dress. She'd insisted on finding a mother-of-the-bride dress with pockets that didn't look like something an "old lady" would wear. She'd succeeded.

Emily held something out to Annie.

Annie burst out laughing when she saw what her mom was holding. A little green plastic Army man. "Tell me that isn't from your wedding," Annie said.

"Of course it is. You were so proud to sprinkle them down the aisle along with the flower petals."

"And you almost fell on your face when you stepped on one," Annie said with a laugh.

"I figured it was apropos to have you carry it on your own wedding day. We can tuck it in with your flowers."

Annie smiled at the thought. "Have I ever said thank you?" she asked.

"For what?" Emily asked.

"For *everything*. For going hungry so I could eat. For protecting me. For letting me ask you a million questions. For letting me play in the dirt and wear pants instead of forcing me to do girly things. For not freaking when I met Frankie and said I wanted to marry him. For being the absolutely best mother anyone could ever ask for. If I can be half the person you are, I'll consider myself a success."

"Oh, honey," Emily said, putting her hands on either side of Annie's face. "You were such an easy child to parent."

Annie snorted.

"You were," her mom insisted. "You could entertain yourself for hours. You were polite and thankful for anything you got. I've always thought I was blessed because you were so empathetic. Anytime you saw someone hurting, your first thought was to try to make them feel better. From Truck and Fish, to Akilah and Tex. You've always wanted to fix others, to heal them. I had no doubt you'd be an amazing soldier, and you were, but you're going to be an even better doctor. I truly believe it's what you were meant to do."

"Mom," Annie said, doing her best to choke back tears.

"And I just want you to know that Frankie is absolutely the man I would choose for you. You know...if I had a say," Emily said with a small chuckle. "He's only ever had eyes for you. Literally. Whenever you were in the same room together, his gaze never left you. If you happened to fall, he was on the move before your father or I even noticed.

He'll be your champion, your cheerleader, and your protector. You can take care of yourself, we both know that, but having a partner you can one hundred percent count on is a blessing."

"You would know," Annie said.

"Yes, I would," Emily agreed.

"Thanks for planning this shindig today," Annie said. "I know I wasn't as much help as I should've been."

Emily shrugged. "It's been fun."

"Did Dad go overboard on security for the reception?"

"Of course he did. He's still pissed those guys dared to rob us during our *own* reception," Emily said.

"Think if I begged, Fish and Tex would recreate their three-legged dance routine?" Annie asked with a chuckle.

"Only if Akilah lets you take her prosthesis to swing like a baseball bat," Emily retorted.

"We've had some good times, haven't we?" Annie asked rhetorically.

"Yeah," Emily answered anyway. "And now I'm sure everyone is waiting for us. Especially Frankie. You have your Green Beret pin, and Aspen's Ranger pin she gave you all those years ago?"

"Yeah, already attached to the edge of my skirt," Annie said.

"Good. I've got your outfit for the reception in the other room. After the ceremony, the photographer is going to want to take some more pictures, since Frankie wasn't allowed to see you until you walk down the aisle. You can change before you two head back to the house."

"Okay, Mom."

"But don't forget to bring your flowers. We'll put them

on the table by the cake. Oh, and I've already tipped the officiant, so you don't have to worry about that."

"Sounds good. Mom, we've—"

Emily didn't give Annie a chance to finish her thought. "Don't feel as if you have to rush to get back to the house. There will be hors d'oeuvres already set up, and of course the open bar, so everyone will be fine until you and Frankie arrive—"

"Mom!"

"What?"

"It'll be fine. Stop worrying."

Emily took a deep breath. "Right. I'm happy for you, Ann Elizabeth Grant Fletcher."

"I'm happy for me too," Annie said.

"Come on, let's put Frankie out of his misery," Emily said. "Your dad was a mess on our wedding day. Kept trying to sneak a glance at me before the ceremony."

Annie smiled as she followed her mom out of the room and back to where everyone was assembling to walk down the aisle. She didn't think Emily would appreciate knowing she and Frankie had already snuck away from their friends earlier and exchanged wedding-day gifts.

Annie had said she was going to the bathroom, with Frankie using the same excuse. They'd hidden out in a storage closet in the church and giggled like naughty kids. Frankie had given her a beautiful diamond bracelet and she'd given him the latest expansion pack for the current version of *This is War*. Harley had pulled some strings to get it early and the excitement in Frankie's eyes when he realized what she'd given him was a joy to see.

They'd made out like teens for a while, and when

Annie figured she'd pushed her luck long enough and if she didn't get back, someone would come looking for her, she'd reluctantly left Frankie in the closet and headed back to the chaos.

When Annie and Emily reentered the room they'd left not ten minutes ago, Rayne yelled, "There you are!"

Everyone began talking at once, the excitement almost crackling in the air. This was hardly the first wedding everyone had been to, but every time someone in their inner circle tied the knot, they all seemed to lose their minds.

When Akilah had married her husband, an Iraqi man she'd met at a mixer for displaced men and women from Iraq, everyone had cried with joy. When Jackson, Wendy's brother, had gotten married, Annie was positive he'd been mortified by everyone's loud enthusiasm. Her family definitely knew how to party, so for herself, Annie was more than looking forward to the reception. There were several people she hadn't gotten to talk to yet and hadn't seen in years, and she couldn't wait to catch up.

But first...she needed to marry the man she loved more than anything else in the world.

CHAPTER SIXTEEN

At the back of the church, waiting with her father and small wedding party, Annie tapped her foot impatiently. The space was separated from the church proper by a set of doors, and she could barely wait for them to open. She was ready to do this. To marry Frankie in front of all their family and friends.

Gillian and Trigger's twins were the flower kids, and they were fidgeting as well, anxious to do their part. It hadn't escaped Annie's notice that there were little green Army men mixed in with the flowers in their baskets.

Fletch leaned close and whispered, "Are you ready for this?"

"I've been ready for this my entire life, Dad," she told him confidently. She had no nerves. Didn't have any second thoughts. She was Frankie's, and he was hers. Period. No questions asked. This marriage was really a formality; they'd pledged themselves to each other years and years ago. And formally, only ten months before on the deck of a sailboat in the Caribbean.

Her dad looked extremely handsome in his tuxedo, as did all his friends. The church was full of "silver foxes," and Annie loved having all her favorite people together in one place.

A noise behind them drew her attention, and Annie glanced over her shoulder to see someone enter the church. For a second, she stood frozen in place, then a huge smile broke out as she strode toward the newcomer, blocking out the organized chaos around her. She vaguely heard the wedding coordinator trying to get everyone's attention, but she didn't stop.

The man who'd entered the church grinned and held out his arms.

Annie walked right into them. "Tex!" she exclaimed happily. "I didn't think you were coming!"

"And miss my favorite girl's wedding? No way!"

Annie sniffed a little as Tex's arms tightened around her. Akilah had already mentioned that her dad was out in California visiting a SEAL who'd been injured in combat, losing both his legs. Tex still worked with injured veterans and did what he could to help them transition to civilian life. Annie was well aware the soldier either had to be very important, or in deep mental anguish for Tex to consider missing her wedding, and that was okay. She wanted him to be where he was needed most.

"Thank you," Annie whispered. She hadn't actually seen Tex since he'd sent the men to rescue them in the Caribbean. She'd thanked him over the phone, but it wasn't the same as doing so in person.

Tex just nodded against her. It was a small miracle he didn't deflect her thanks or protest he hadn't done anything. He wasn't known for graciously accepting gratitude.

Annie pulled back and took in the man who had a bigger savior complex than anyone she'd ever met. He'd single-handedly taken it upon himself to keep his friends' women safe. And their kids. And their friends. Annie had no idea how many people this man had under his wing, but she was grateful to be one of the many. She'd always known that he tracked people, and that he had some scary skills when it came to technology, but she'd never been as glad to have him at her back as she was on that island.

"I knew the second our names were listed in a computer somewhere as 'missing,' you'd send in the troops," she told him quietly. "And I appreciate you letting me and Frankie continue our vacation."

He scowled. "It's a good thing you didn't send cards and flowers every day for a year as a thank you," Tex said.

Annie grinned. She *knew* Tex would see the footage from the soldiers who'd rescued them. "I know better than that," she told him.

"Hey, Daddy," Akilah said from behind them.

Tex's eyes lit up when he saw his daughter. He kissed Annie on the forehead and said, "Remind me to give you my wedding present before I leave."

"I can't wait to see what kind of tracking device you've come up with now," Annie deadpanned.

Tex laughed, then turned to Akilah. Seeing how much love Tex had for his adopted daughter made Annie sigh. Maybe she was feeling extra-sentimental, since it was her wedding day, but she adored witnessing the easy affection he wasn't afraid to show to his daughter. Akilah was in her mid-thirties, married, and with a child of her own, and yet Tex still treated her as if she was the second-most-precious thing in his life.

Second only because everyone knew Tex lived and breathed for his wife, Melody. He'd do anything for her. Literally *anything*. Break laws, crack skulls, call in every marker he'd ever earned. No one fucked with his Melody. No one.

And speaking of his wife, she appeared as if out of nowhere.

"John!" she exclaimed. "I wasn't sure you'd make it!" Melody said.

Akilah stepped back with a smile as Tex greeted his wife. They'd been together for decades, but Tex still looked at Melody as if she was the most beautiful woman in the world and the only person in the room.

"Hey, Mel. I wasn't sure I'd make it either, but if I missed Annie's wedding, Fletch would never let me live it down." They kissed gently, and Annie smiled seeing the love between them.

"We need to get this ceremony moving, otherwise your groom is gonna lose his mind," the wedding coordinator said from nearby.

"Sorry," Tex apologized. "I didn't mean to slow things down."

Annie snorted.

"Did you just snort at me, young lady?" Tex asked.

Annie wiped the smirk from her face. "Of course not."

Tex shook his head and wrapped his arm around Melody. "Right." Then he kissed Akilah on the temple and opened one of the doors, walking into the church proper with his wife.

Annie heard him announce loudly, "Sorry, not Annie. Just an old man and his beautiful wife," as the door quietly closed behind them.

The laughter from all the guests was easy to hear.

Leave it to Tex to make an entrance.

She felt an arm go around her waist and looked up at her dad. "Did you know Tex was going to be here?"

"He told me he'd be cutting it close. But I knew he'd definitely be at the reception."

"Here's hoping he doesn't have to use his prosthetic as a weapon like he did at your reception, huh?" Annie teased.

Fletch shivered. "Seeing you swing Akilah's arm at that one asshole was enough to give me nightmares for years," he said.

Annie grinned. "I vaguely remember doing that, but mostly, all I recall is having the time of my life. I was so happy you and Mom were getting married and that everyone was so nice."

"Come on, let's put this poor wedding coordinator out of her misery and get you to Frankie, all right?"

Annie nodded. "Definitely all right."

Fletch gave the frazzled coordinator a chin lift, and the woman visibly sighed in relief. Annie wasn't concerned that things were just a bit chaotic. With friends and family like hers, she expected nothing different.

Frankie stood at the front of the church with his eyes fixed on the doors. He wasn't nervous. Not in the least. He was excited. He couldn't wait to see Annie, despite managing to steal her away for a private moment just hours ago.

He was proud to claim her in front of all their family and friends, and more importantly, to have her claim *him*. There was a time as a child when he didn't think he was worthy of being loved. His own mother had shunned him because of his disability. But with the help of his teacher—now his godmother—and her husband, Cooper, he'd started to realize maybe he wasn't as awful as he felt.

All his life, he'd wanted to be a husband. Wanted to be *Annie's* husband. So many people had tried to convince him that what he'd felt for her since the age of seven wasn't true love. But he knew deep in his heart that it was, all along.

He saw Tex enter through the doors at the back of the room, thrilled that the man had made it. Annie would never know how often he and Tex talked, especially when she was deployed. Tex had reassured him that Annie was all right more than once. He'd never be able to repay him for that.

Frankie didn't hear what Tex said to the room, but everyone in attendance laughed. He loved that their ceremony was full of joy. When Joe and Josie came down the aisle sprinkling flowers and Army men, everyone laughed again, and he could hear whispers from some of the people who knew the history behind the toys, most likely explaining to others.

Akilah and Cooper appeared next. After several conversations with Emily, he and Annie had convinced her mom that they didn't need traditional bridesmaids and groomsmen. But since Annie and Akilah were close, Annie had wanted her friend involved in some way. And Cooper had literally saved his life when he was in elementary school, and was one of the first people—after Frankie's dad and teacher—to make him feel okay about his disability.

So Akilah and Cooper were the next to come down the aisle, behind Gillian's twins. They walked arm in arm, and the sight of Akilah kicking aside little plastic Army men, ensuring Annie didn't trip on her way down the aisle, made him smile.

When the music changed to Mendelssohn's "Wedding March," everyone in the church stood and turned to face the doors. Frankie held his breath as he waited for his Annie to appear.

The doors opened one last time, and he inhaled sharply when he saw the woman he loved. She was beaming, one arm looped around Fletch's. They began walking down the aisle slowly, and Frankie couldn't take his eyes off her.

She was so damn beautiful, it made his heart hurt. He'd known her dress was dark green, but he never imagined how stunning she'd look.

Some people would think it was a pity she didn't dress this nice every day. But Frankie loved Annie no matter how she looked. He loved her when her hair was in tangles and her face was covered in dirt and sweat. He loved her when she was exhausted, with dark circles under her eyes. He loved her when she wore pants, shorts, dresses, or nothing at all.

He loved Annie because of who she was inside. Kind,

tough as nails, stubborn, funny, generous, and outgoing. Watching her sweep down the aisle was like watching a royal princess greeting her constituents, except she knew each and every person she acknowledged with a smile as she continued toward him.

Fletch escorted Annie to the stairs leading to where Frankie was standing, and he walked down to meet them. He held out his hand to Fletch and the man took it. Uncharacteristically, he squeezed Frankie's fingers tightly and leaned in for a hug, not letting his hand drop.

When he got close, Fletch said softly, "I'm not *giving* my daughter to you. I'm entrusting her into your care. There's a difference. Don't ever make me regret it."

Then he pulled back and smiled as if he hadn't just issued a subtle threat.

"Dad, what the hell did you just say?" Annie demanded.

"Nothing, sprite. Just welcoming Frankie to the family," Fletch said innocently.

Frankie wasn't upset or surprised by Fletch's warning. He was pleased Annie had someone else so protective at her back. He nodded to Fletch, acknowledging his words.

Fletch hesitated for just a second, then placed Annie's hand over Frankie's.

The second he turned to walk to his place in the front pew next to Emily and the rest of his family, Annie whispered, "What did he say?"

"Nothing I wouldn't say to the person marrying my daughter." Frankie tucked Annie's hand in the crook of his elbow and turned to head up to the altar.

"Wait, now we're having kids?" Annie teased.

At the altar, Frankie turned and looked down at Annie.

His heart thudded forcefully in his chest and he couldn't stop grinning.

She smiled back and brought a hand to his chest. "You look amazing," she whispered.

Frankie didn't care that they were having this moment in front of over a hundred people. He didn't care they were holding up the ceremony. All he cared about was the woman in front of him. "As do you."

"Look," Annie said, pulling up the hem of her dress. Her combat boots sparkled even in the muted lighting of the church.

"They're perfect," Frankie told her. Then he gestured to his own feet, to show her that he too wore combat boots, although his didn't have hundreds of shiny sparkles.

Annie giggled.

"I figured I'd see what all the fuss was all about," Frankie went on. "I mean, you love them and wear them all the time, so I figured they had to be comfortable."

"Are they?" Annie asked.

Frankie leaned forward and whispered, "No."

Annie threw her head back and laughed. Frankie just stared, thanking his lucky stars that this day had finally arrived. When she had herself under control Annie said, "You have to break them in. They get better, I promise."

The officiant cleared her throat and Frankie suddenly remembered where they were. "Wanna get married?"

"Again?" Annie asked with a smile.

"Yeah."

"Sure. I don't have anything else to do right this moment," she teased.

They turned to the officiant and Frankie nodded at her to begin.

"We are gathered here today to celebrate the joining of this man and woman..."

All too soon, it was time to exchange vows.

"Do you, Franklin Sanders, take Ann Elizabeth Grant Fletcher to be your lawfully wedded wife? To have and hold from this day forward, for better, for worse, for richer, for poorer, in sickness and health, to love and to cherish, till death do you part?"

"I do," Frankie said without hesitation.

"Do you, Ann Elizabeth Grant Fletcher, take Franklin Sanders to be your lawfully wedded husband? To have and hold from this day forward, for better, for worse, for richer, for poorer, in sickness and health, to love and to cherish, till death do you part?"

"I definitely do," Annie said with enthusiasm.

"You may now share your own vows," the woman said.

Frankie and Annie had talked about this. They wanted to make the ceremony their own, but as far as they were concerned, they'd already said their true vows on that ship in the Caribbean.

"Today, in front of our family and friends, I'm blessed to have my dream come true," Frankie told Annie. "I might not be the richest man, or the smartest, or the most coordinated, but I am the *only* man in the world who will always put you first. Who will move heaven and earth to give you what you need and desire. I will protect you with my life, kill all the spiders who dare invade our home, and gladly cook for both of us for the rest of our days."

Frankie waited for the laughter to die down before he continued.

"I'm perfectly aware of how lucky I am," he said. "Every day, I pinch myself that you're with me. I'll never take you for granted and will endeavor to show you each and every minute how much I love you."

Annie smiled at him, then mumbled, "I thought we weren't going to get all emotional?"

Frankie shrugged. "Can't help it," he told her.

Annie took a deep breath and began speaking. "It's always been you, Frankie. From the moment I saw you, something deep within me said, 'This is the man you'll marry.' I'm not the most graceful person in the world, I'm too loud, too forceful, too opinionated, too tomboyish. But I love you with everything that I am. I've had the best examples of what love is all around me, my entire life. Love is unselfish. Love is saying 'I'm sorry,' love is going to a seafood restaurant when you're really in the mood for a hamburger. You're my best friend; the last person I want to talk to at night and the first I want to see in the morning. I can't wait to see what our life brings us."

Frankie squeezed Annie's hands and they both turned to the officiant. They went through the tradition of exchanging bands and when they were properly ringed up, the officiant continued, "By the power vested in me, I now pronounce you husband and wife. You may kiss your bride."

Annie asked, "How about if I kiss my husband instead?" Then she reached up, wrapped her hand around the back of Frankie's neck, and pulled him close.

Frankie heard laughter before he closed his eyes and

enjoyed kissing his wife. Both very aware of who was watching them, they kept their passion in check. When they turned to face everyone, Annie held their clasped hands up and let out a loud *whoop*.

Everyone laughed and cheered as Annie practically pulled him down the aisle, smiling and greeting everyone she didn't get the chance to welcome before the ceremony.

Two hours later, after they'd greeted every single person, signed the official marriage documents, had a million more pictures taken, and had changed into casual clothes for the reception, Frankie finally had a second to sit down with Annie. They were in the same room where she'd gotten dressed earlier. They were alone, the limo waiting outside to take them to her parents' house. But first Frankie wanted a moment with his wife.

He handed her a rolled-up piece of paper.

Annie looked down in confusion. "What's this?"

"Tex slipped it to me before he left," Frankie said, skirting around the question.

"He's gonna be at the reception, isn't he?" Annie asked.

"As far as I know. Open it and let's see what it is," he replied.

"Shit. It could be anything," Annie said, staring down at the tightly rolled document. "The deed to a new house. Five million dollars worth of stock shares. A notarized document saying that I promise to name my firstborn after him."

Frankie chuckled. "Go on, open it."

"You know what this is, don't you?" Annie accused.

"Maybe. You would too if you shut up and unrolled it."

Annie rolled her eyes, but swiped the rubber band

down the paper. She unfurled the document and stared at it for a long moment, reading.

Finally, her gaze met his. "Is this what I think it is?"

"If you think it's an official Bahamian marriage license with all the proper signatures, making the ceremony we had ten months ago perfectly legal here in the United States? Then yes."

"Holy shit! How in the hell did Tex know?"

Frankie laughed. "Did you seriously just ask that?"

"Right, stupid question. But...we didn't go through the proper channels. We were supposed to turn in all the documents before we actually got married."

Frankie shrugged. "I don't know or care how he did it, I'm just over-the-moon happy that he did."

"Does this mean we're bigamists?" Annie asked.

Frankie's brows furrowed even as he laughed. "What?"

"I mean, if we were already married, and we just got married again, is that even legal?"

"Who cares." Frankie shrugged with a huge smile. "Besides, now we can celebrate our anniversary twice every year."

"And get twice as many presents." Annie winked.

"Take twice as many vacations," Frankie added.

"A reason to have wild monkey sex twice as much," Annie replied with a smile.

"We need a reason?" Frankie asked.

"True." Annie rolled the certificate and carefully put the rubber band back around it. "This must've been what Tex was talking about when he saw me before I walked down the aisle." She put the document aside and straddled Frankie's lap. He was sitting on a small settee, and he put his hands on her hips to keep her firmly in place. "I love you," Annie told him.

"Not as much as I love you."

"Think we can skip this little party and head home early?" Annie asked.

Frankie snorted. "Um. No."

"Just asking," Annie said with a grin.

Frankie knew for a fact that Annie didn't want to miss the reception. There were too many people she wanted to catch up with. He ran a hand over her hair. It was mussed now, and she was wearing a black scoop-neck T-shirt with a pair of khaki pants. And her sparkly combat boots. Everyone had been instructed to change into something comfortable for their reception, just like her mom and dad had done twenty or so years ago.

Annie was just as beautiful now as she was two hours ago, when he'd seen her in the gorgeous green dress. He *did* want to take her home. Show her exactly how much he loved her. Worship her. Make sure she knew how appreciative he was that she'd married him today. But there would be plenty of time to make love to his wife. They had their entire lives ahead of them.

"What?" Annie asked when he didn't say anything.

"Nothing," Frankie said. "Just trying to get up the energy to stand and go smile for the next six hours or so."

"Four," Annie said decisively.

"Four what?"

"Hours. We'll cut the cake. Dance. Talk. But come ten o'clock. We're out of there."

"Deal," Frankie said. They had a reservation at a bed and breakfast about fifteen minutes away and would be spending the night there. Tomorrow, they would return to her parents' house for brunch, then head back down to Austin so Annie could get ready for her classes in the upcoming week. They had no plans to take a honeymoon; they both considered their sailing trip their official honeymoon.

"One of us has to move," Annie said after a minute or two.

Sighing, Frankie nodded as if he was extremely put out, then he stood with Annie in his arms. She didn't screech or grab onto him, afraid he'd drop her. She merely snuggled into his chest as if she had all the faith in the world in him.

"You ready for the crazy that's about to happen?" Frankie asked when they were both settled in the limo and on the way to her parents' house.

Annie nodded, but said, "No."

Frankie kissed her lightly and stroked the rings on her left ring finger. "The best day of my life was the day I met you."

"Same," Annie whispered, before kissing him again.

They spent the rest of the short trip to the Fletchers' house making out, then trying to smooth down their hair and make themselves presentable before greeting all their guests.

"Do I look okay?" Annie asked, biting her lip as they waited for their driver to walk around the car and open the door.

Her cheeks were flushed, her lips were a bit swollen from their kisses, and her shirt was askew, but all Frankie could say was, "You're perfect."

The noise of everyone greeting them as the door opened was loud. Frankie just smiled. He loved this. All of it. Annie was loved by so many people, and while there were some here for him, like his dad and Cooper and Kiera, most of the guests were there because of Annie. Frankie kissed her temple. "Ready?"

"Ready," she said confidently. "Together, we can face anything. Even a big-ass party put on by my mom and her crazy friends."

Hand-in-hand, Mr. and Mrs. Sanders climbed out of the limo and headed to their reception.

CHAPTER SEVENTEEN

Annie couldn't stop smiling. Everyone was having an amazing time. Laughing, catching up, dancing. She and Frankie had eaten dinner, posed for more pictures, cut their cake, done the obligatory first dance, and now she finally had some time to walk around and talk to people she'd known her entire life.

Every now and then, she'd look around for Frankie, and each and every time she found his eyes on her. They were truly soul mates, drawn to each other even when they weren't standing side-by-side. This was what she'd always wanted, what she'd grown up seeing with her parents and all their friends. That almost supernatural connection was something she'd craved, and she'd found it with Frankie.

She'd already thanked Tex for getting the Bahamian marriage certificate. She'd asked how many laws he'd broken to secure it, but he'd kept his mouth shut, telling her not to worry about it.

Her brother Ethan was there with his girlfriend from college, Doug was hanging out with two of his friends who'd been invited, and John was playing cards with some of the sons of the other Delta members her dad had gotten close to over the years.

There were a few people Annie didn't know, and even she was surprised to see how many children were in attendance. She'd been so busy thinking about making it from one mission to the next, she hadn't really thought about having kids of her own someday. But now, she couldn't *stop* thinking about it.

Did she want kids? She thought she did. A rough-and-tumble little boy to whom she could pass on her love of obstacle courses, who her dad could spoil rotten and all his friends could brainwash into wanting to join the Army. Yeah, she could live with that.

Speaking of her dad's friends, her unofficial uncles, Annie headed for the man she hadn't gotten to talk to yet. Truck. He was sitting at a table off to the side, his gaze locked on his wife, Mary. She and Rayne were laughing their heads off at who knew what near the bar.

Truck had a half smile on his face, and it was easy to see the love in his eyes.

"Hey, stranger," Annie said as she approached.

Truck's head swung around and the half smile morphed into a full one. "Annie!" he exclaimed and stood. He wrapped his arms around her in a bear hug and held on tightly for a long moment. "Congratulations," he said when he let go.

"Thanks. I feel bad that I haven't had a chance to even say hello to you until now."

Truck waved off her apology. "You've been a bit busy," he said dryly.

"True." Annie pulled out a chair and they both sat. She rested her head on her hand and stared at the man who was nearly as much a father to her as Fletch had been.

"You know, this almost reminds me of your dad's reception," Truck said.

"Without the guns and mayhem, you mean?" Annie quipped.

"Yeah. That," he said with a laugh. "But seriously, with everyone dressed down, the sound of kids laughing, you looking so much like your mom...It's nice."

It *was* nice. Annie agreed. "You and Mary look good," she said. "How're your kids?"

"They were sorry they couldn't be here," Truck said. "Ford has a killer schedule this year at college, all advanced classes, and he's determined to get on the honor roll. I keep telling him that we don't expect him to get all A's, but he's determined."

Annie chuckled.

"And Elizabeth is at band camp this week. She felt horrible for missing your wedding, but since she's a senior, and one of the field commanders, she couldn't really skip it."

"It's okay," Annie said. "I'm sorry I didn't get to see them, but I'm sure we'll get together the next time we're all in town."

Truck nodded absently. "How did I get so old?" he muttered.

Annie blinked. "You're not old."

Truck just shook his head. "I am. I remember when we used to let you run over us in that tank of yours. Hell, I remember when you and Frankie met like it was yesterday.

You sold your Army man to buy him that thingamabob for his iPad so you guys could talk to each other, and *he* sold his iPad to buy you a case for your Army man." Truck shook his head. "You two have always been meant for each other."

Annie nodded. She was very glad her mom and Frankie's godmother, Kiera, had the foresight to not actually sell their kids' prized possessions. So Annie had gotten the plastic cases for her Army men, and Frankie had gotten the technology they'd needed to talk to each other when he went home.

"I remember when I first met you," Annie said softly. "You were huge and sitting in a chair in Fletch's backyard. I was hungry and scared for my mom, and you were doing everything in your power not to scare me with your size."

"Yup. And you crawled right up into my lap, put your hand over the scar on my face, and asked if it hurt. You had me wrapped around your little finger from the very start."

"Thank you for teaching me what love *really* is," Annie told him, not giving him a chance to respond before continuing. "It's putting the other person first, no matter what. It's loving them even when they aren't perfect. It's protecting them when they can't protect themselves. But most of all, it's loving unconditionally. You and Mary are my idols. At first glance, you don't seem to be compatible. But out of all Dad's teammates, you two are probably the most connected."

"She's my everything," Truck said simply. Then he pinned Annie with his intense gaze. "I'm proud of you."

Four words were all it took to make Annie tear up. She

respected this man so much, and she couldn't remember him ever telling her that before.

"You were a hell of a soldier and an even better Special Forces operative. Our country lost one of their best Green Berets when you chaptered out, but I have no doubt that you made the right decision. Every time I had to leave Mary and our kids behind when I went on a mission, I worried nonstop about what would happen to them if I didn't come home. We both know the odds of all of us surviving our tours is damn low. I always thought Mary deserved better, especially after everything she'd been through and what she'd survived. Sometimes the easy decision is to stick with what you know, and in your case, that was being in the Army and being a Green Beret. But the harder decision is to make a leap and do something new. You're gonna be an amazing doctor, Annie, and Frankie will sleep easier, knowing you aren't putting your life on the line anymore."

Annie pressed her lips together and nodded. "I worried about you guys, and my dad, but I didn't truly understand the odds you faced until I was in your shoes."

Truck nodded. "You can't look back, sprite," he said, using her nickname. "You can only go forward. You and Frankie have that something special. That spark. That connection. You'll survive whatever life throws at you. I have no doubt about that."

"I hope so."

"I know so," Truck said. Then he gave someone behind her a chin lift.

Annie turned, expecting to see her dad or one of her many honorary uncles, but instead it was Frankie.

"You okay?" he asked a little gruffly.

Confused, Annie nodded.

"I saw you crying," he explained. "I just wanted to make sure everything was all right."

Annie's heart melted. She stood and plastered herself to her husband. "Truck was being mushy," she explained.

Frankie lifted an eyebrow skeptically, and Annie heard Truck chuckling behind her at the reaction. "I know, I know, it's an anomaly, but it happened."

"Okay. Can I get you anything? You want another glass of champagne?"

"I'm good. Thanks."

"All right. And just to warn you...your dad is feeling nostalgic and went to the garage to unearth that damn tank," Frankie said.

Annie rolled her eyes, but secretly she was excited. She loved that thing, had ridden it until she was in her late teens. She'd jump at another chance to take it for a lap around the yard.

"And your mom said she has a present for us," Frankie continued.

"Another one?" Annie asked. Her mom had already been too generous. She needed to have a word with her and tell her to stop already.

"Apparently."

"Go on," Truck said as he stood. "I need to check on Mary anyway." He bent, kissed the top of Annie's head, gave Frankie another chin lift, then turned to leave. When he was a few feet away, he stopped and turned back. "Good job on keeping an eye on your wife." Then he walked away once more.

Frankie merely shook his head. "Your dad's friends scare me sometimes, but they're damn good men."

"They are," Annie agreed. "Shall we go find my mom and see what she's got for us now? We have," she brought her left arm up and made an exaggerated point of checking the time, "one hour and twenty-three minutes until we're leaving."

Frankie grabbed her wrist and turned her hand over, kissing her palm before lacing their fingers together. "Yup."

They walked across the yard, stopping several times to talk to more people, before they found Annie's mom.

"Hey, Mom, Frankie said you wanted to see me?" Annie asked.

"Yes. Come inside. Both of you," Emily said.

Annie and Frankie followed her mom into the house and up the stairs to her room. Sitting on the bed were two of Annie's most prized possessions. Except they looked very different than the last time she'd seen them.

Annie looked at her mom, tears already filling her eyes. "Mom?"

"They're your Army men. The ones Fletch gave you when he first met us. And yes, those are the same plastic cases Frankie gave you, but I took the liberty of taking them to a collector shop and asking them to do what they could to clean them up. They were scratched and scuffed pretty badly, as you know."

Annie walked to the bed and picked up one of the cases. She'd left the dolls with her parents when she'd gone to college. She hadn't wanted to be made fun of, and after graduating, hadn't wanted to risk losing them when they moved from post to post. She'd meant to ask her mom about them several times, but with how busy she'd been lately, it slipped her mind.

Even though it had been ten years since she'd seen the dolls, memories of how much they'd meant to her were almost overwhelming.

Frankie came up next to her and picked up the second doll. He'd taken one of them back with him to California after they'd met, and they'd spent many hours playing with the dolls—still in the plastic containers, of course—over the Internet. He'd brought his back to Annie when she'd graduated from high school, so they could be stored together at her parents' house.

"They still look brand-new," he commented.

"Right?" Emily asked. "And I'll have you know the guy at the shop was drooling over them. Said that if you ever wanted to sell them, he'd pay top dollar."

"Sell them? Not a chance," Annie said. "You wouldn't sell them when we were practically starving; no way in hell I'd ever part with them now."

Fletch entered the room, obviously having seen them sneak into the house. He curled an arm around Emily's waist, gently resting his chin on top of her head. "I remember the day I gave those to you like it was yesterday," he said. "You were so thrilled and proud to have a new toy, it broke my heart."

"And mine," Emily added.

"I wasn't just that," Annie insisted, putting the plastic case down on the bed and going over to her parents. "Yes, the newness was cool, but it was because *Fletch* had given them to me. I remember being a little scared of men. So many had been mean to me, but not you. You answered my questions and treated me as if I was important. It was because they were a gift from a man I'd come to admire and look up to. And because they weren't girl toys. You understood me. Even back then. That's part of the reason why they meant so much."

"Ah, sprite," Fletch said, then pressed his lips together tightly, not saying anything else. It was obvious he was trying to hold onto his composure.

"Well, now you can take them home. And maybe when you have kids of your own, you can finally take them out of their plastic prisons and set them free," Annie's mom said with a gleam in her eye.

"Mom! Seriously? We've been married like two seconds and you're already angling for grandkids?"

"Yup," Emily said without remorse. "Your brothers are too young. And you aren't getting any younger."

"Jeez, it's not like I'm getting gray hair or anything yet," Annie complained.

"Your mom has baby fever," Fletch said. "John's getting to the age where he thinks his parents are stupid and would rather hang out with his buds all the time. And none of her friends have young kids anymore. Joe and Josie do in a pinch, but she doesn't get to see Gillian and Trigger enough. So..."

Annie rolled her eyes. "I need to get through med school before I even think about kids," she said firmly.

"I can wait a year or so," Emily said smugly.

Annie didn't want to break it to her mom that med school took a hell of a lot longer than a year. Not to mention the years of residency and possible fellowships.

"Fletch! Are you up there? Come on, man! We got the tank going!" Coach yelled from downstairs.

Annie laughed. "Seriously, Dad?"

Fletch smirked. "You know you want to take a turn."

"Take a turn?" Annie asked. "It's my tank, I get to take the *first* turn!" Then she ran down the stairs, laughing as she tried to stay ahead of her dad, who was crowding behind her.

———

Emily shook her head, watching her daughter's husband. Frankie was staring at the door where Annie had disappeared, a small smile on his face.

"Thank you for making her so happy," Emily said gently.

"Thank *you* for raising such a wonderful woman," Frankie countered.

Then they smiled at each other, before Frankie turned back to the bed to look at the dolls. "I can't believe the cases cleaned up so well."

"The guy who worked on them *did* tell me one of the dolls wasn't quite as pristine as the other," she said with a grin.

Frankie shrugged, completely unfazed. "Yeah, I took the one I had out of its packaging, but only when I wasn't on the computer with Annie. I played with that thing all the time. My dad bought me additional clothes for it because I knew if I damaged the original uniform it came with, Annie would lose her mind."

Emily laughed. He wasn't wrong. "You're a good man to overlook her...quirks," she said.

"Annie's quirks are what make her so amazing," Frankie said with a shrug.

"Your secret is safe with me," Emily reassured him. "He also found a note tucked into the box," she said, walking to her dresser, then handing him a folded piece of paper.

Frankie took it from her and smiled. "Did you read it?"

"Would you think badly of your mother-in-law if I admitted that I did?" Emily asked.

Frankie laughed and shook his head. "No."

"Then yeah, I totally read it," Emily admitted.

"I, Frankie Sanders, declare that I'm going to marry Annie Fletcher someday," Frankie recited without opening the small piece of paper. "I love her more than peanut butter and jelly and I'll do whatever it takes to make her love me the same way." He knew exactly what was on that piece of paper, since he'd written it. "I was a dork," he said dryly.

"I think that's the most romantic thing I've ever seen," Emily countered.

"I wrote it when I was eight or so. Annie had been talking to me over my iPad for about a year. She gave me the confidence I needed to be more outgoing, the courage to agree to the cochlear implant. I've loved her forever, and I promise I'll protect and love her for the rest of my life."

Emily smiled. "I know you will."

Frankie fingered the note, then put it in his back pocket. "I'm sure when Annie gets done terrorizing everyone with her driving skills, she'll want these to go back home with us."

"I'll find a bag for them and put them with your other wedding gifts," Emily said. "Tomorrow when you're here for brunch, we'll get everything loaded into your SUV."

"I appreciate it."

They heard loud laughter coming from the backyard, and Emily huffed out a breath. "Go on, you better go supervise your wife. She tends to get a little competitive, especially around the guys."

Frankie walked over and hugged her before leaving the room, Emily staying where she was for a moment. Her and Annie's life had been hard when she'd been a single mother, but she'd always done what she thought was best for her daughter. She still pinched herself when she thought about how lucky she'd been to meet the man of her dreams. Fletch had shown her what love truly was, and had taken Annie under his wing as if she was his own.

Sometimes it was hard to believe her little girl was a grown adult, and a lethal Special Forces operative in her own right. But as long as Annie was happy, Emily was content.

When she heard another scream and lots of laughter, she turned for the door. She didn't want to miss another second of whatever mayhem was going on in the yard. Making sure she had her phone in her pocket so she could record the craziness, Emily smiled all the way down the stairs and out the door.

EPILOGUE

Ten Years Later

"No!" the little girl shouted, stomping her foot for good measure. "I want to wear my princess dress! And crown. And jewels."

Annie sighed and sat back on her heels. She was in the middle of her daughter's room, trying to get her dressed so they could head out for her parents' house. They were already thirty minutes late leaving since earlier, Melanie wouldn't get out of the tub.

"Melanie Emily Sanders, come over here right now," Annie said in her "mom" voice.

Three-year-old Melanie pouted but shuffled over to where her mom was sitting.

"We're going to see Grammy and PopPop. It's chilly outside. Your legs will freeze if you wear a dress," Annie explained.

But her stubborn little monster shook her head and her lip began to tremble.

Annie felt Frankie's hand on her shoulder a split second before he spoke.

"How about instead of the princess dress, you wear your pink tutu, the one with the sparkles? And the pink buttery-soft leggings. You like those because they aren't scratchy, right? And they'll match the tutu."

"Yeah!" Melanie shouted happily, running straight to her closet, which was full of more pink and sparkles than Annie had ever seen in her life.

Standing, Annie sagged into Frankie and rested her forehead against his. "If I didn't give birth to her, I'd definitely wonder if she was my biological child," Annie mused.

Frankie chuckled and ran a hand over her hair. He kissed her cheek before pulling back. "Why don't you go and make sure we've got enough snacks for the trip to your parents' place? We both know five minutes after we pull out of the driveway, our daughter is gonna be hungry."

"True. Oh, and she wants to take the purple purse today. You know, the one my mom gave her for Christmas. And don't forget to put at least two different ChapSticks in there."

"You know she's gonna want to wear makeup by the time she's ten, right?" Frankie asked with a grin.

"Seriously, how can two people be so completely different?" Annie mused. "She refused to get out of the tub because she kept saying she was still dirty. When I was her age, I threw a fit if I had to get *into* the bathtub. I much preferred to be dirty than to wash my face or comb my hair. And she's constantly putting ChapStick on, pretending it's lipstick. Where did I go wrong?" she griped.

Frankie laughed again, then walked Annie to their daughter's bedroom door. After glancing over at Melanie—who was preoccupied with her clothes and not paying any attention to her mom and dad—Frankie leaned down and kissed her. It wasn't one of his short, fast pecks either.

Annie melted into her husband. He was the only one who could manage to calm her down so easily. He was still her rock. Her cheerleader, study partner, and best friend. Med school had been the hardest thing Annie had ever done. Even more difficult than becoming a Green Beret. There were times when she didn't think she was going to make it. But Frankie would give her a pep talk, remind her of how much she'd already accomplished and how far she'd come, and she'd be good to go again.

She was now working at one of the busiest emergency rooms in Austin. Every day was an adventure, bringing her new cases and making sure she didn't get complacent or bored. Annie worked long, weird hours, but she knew without a doubt her husband and daughter were safe and happy.

Frankie had scaled back his hours, only working part-time at the VA hospital now. He still met with disabled veterans and helped them acclimate to a hearing world after they lost their own, but his greatest joy in life was staying home with Melanie.

Annie had never seen two people connect on such a deep level. Melanie loved her mom, but she *adored* her daddy. Mel was fairly fluent in sign language by the time she was two and was fascinated with Frankie's speech processor. She had a meltdown a few months ago because she wanted one too, and when her dad explained that she didn't need one because her ears worked perfectly, Melanie moped for weeks.

Annie stared at Frankie and licked her lips. She loved this man so much. When they'd made the decision to try for a child, she wasn't sure how successful they'd be. Annie wasn't exactly young anymore, and she'd been on birth control for years. But to her surprise, she was pregnant just a couple months later.

Everyone had been overjoyed when she'd had a little girl. Annie had visions of teaching her to run the obstacle courses she'd loved so much as a child, playing in the dirt, and generally having a mini-me. But that wasn't what she'd gotten. She'd gotten a little girl who pitched a fit when she had to wear jeans because they were "scratchy." When she was given a blue sticker at daycare, she cried because it was a "boy" color.

Melanie loved dolls and stuffed animals and nine times out of ten, preferred to wear dresses. She also hated to be dirty. When she was one, and they'd put a giant birthday cake in front of her, Melanie had cried when she got icing on her hand and couldn't get it off.

Her parents didn't help any, either. They were constantly buying their granddaughter poofy skirts, shirts with sparkles, and crafts that used glitter. Annie would never get the damn glitter out of her carpet and off her floors. Just when she thought she'd vacuumed up the worst of the stuff, more appeared out of nowhere.

"This one, Daddy!" Melanie exclaimed from behind

them.

Frankie and Annie turned to see her holding up a purple sequined crop top she'd worn that summer in her tiny-tots dance recital.

Annie groaned.

Frankie laughed. "Go on, I'll get her into something more appropriate," he said. Then he licked his lips and asked softly, "You think Fletch and your mom will mind if we dropped her off and headed to that bed and breakfast immediately?"

Annie could see the lust in her husband's eyes, and her belly clenched. Even after all the years they'd been together, their sex life hadn't waned. "They'll be thrilled," Annie told him.

"Good." Frankie kissed her quickly, then gave her a small push into the hall. "Go. We'll be down soon."

"Good luck," Annie said as she headed for the stairs. She heard Frankie talking to their daughter as she went. He was an amazing father. Loving, but not a pushover. Strict, but not afraid to get silly with Melanie either. He'd given their daughter a love of books, and every night he lay in bed and read to her.

Melanie might be as different from her as night and day, but Annie wouldn't change her daughter for anything in the world. Even though she didn't always understand her quirks and it was hard to relate to her ultra-girliness, she felt blessed. Melanie was healthy, smart, outgoing, and never met someone she didn't like. Just the other day, when Annie came home after a long shift, her daughter was talking about a boy in her daycare class who was in a wheelchair. Mason was the topic of conversation all evening, and when Frankie had lifted an eyebrow at her over their daughter's head, Annie couldn't help but laugh.

She totally wouldn't be surprised if Melanie and this Mason boy ended up together one day. Just like she and Frankie had.

Annie had always respected and loved her mom, but now that she was a mother herself, she understood keenly the sacrifices Emily had made all those years ago. Annie would do anything for her daughter. Would definitely go hungry if it meant giving Melanie food to eat. Would protect her daughter with her life. Some of her best moments were the tea parties with Melanie and her stuffed animals and dolls, or snuggling with her and watching a princess movie for the millionth time.

Annie grabbed some cheese sticks from the refrigerator and quickly peeled an orange and put it in a plastic bag. She added a drink box and some goldfish crackers to the stash of snacks, and after she'd packaged them up, along with plenty of napkins and wet wipes so Melanie could clean up after she ate, Annie paused, staring out the window over the sink in the kitchen.

Sometimes she had to pinch herself that this was her life. She had a husband who loved her madly, and who she loved back. She had a daughter who was precocious and constantly kept her on her toes. She had a beautiful house and a job she absolutely adored. She was making a difference in her community, helping to save the lives of the patients who came in with severe trauma. Her parents were healthy and didn't mind babysitting their granddaughter when Annie and Frankie needed a small break.

She turned her head and smiled at the two plastic

Army dolls encased in their boxes. They were sitting on a shelf Frankie had made himself and installed in a place of honor in their living room. She was blessed, and so damn thankful that her parents had encouraged her friendship with the little deaf boy she'd met when she was seven. Without their support, who knew where she'd be today? Definitely not this blissfully happy. Annie knew that without a doubt.

"Mommy!" Melanie yelled as she clomped down the stairs. "I ready!"

Annie turned to see her daughter stepping down the last stair into the living room. She wore fuzzy socks and the plastic heels that came with one of the costumes Fletch had given her for her birthday that year. A pink tutu dress, pink leggings, and the purple crop top was worn over a pink long-sleeve shirt. She had her little girl purse over one shoulder and was holding a huge peacock feather she'd gotten the last time they'd visited the zoo.

She looked ridiculous—and so damn cute. Annie could only shake her head.

Frankie shrugged and signed over their daughter's head. *She wouldn't take no for an answer about the top. But I managed to convince her to wear the shirt underneath so she doesn't freeze.*

There were two suitcases in the back of their SUV, so Grammy and PopPop would have plenty of clothes to choose from. When Melanie decided on what she wanted to wear, that was it. Most of the time it was easier to just go with it than try to convince her otherwise.

And secretly, Annie loved that her daughter had such

strong opinions. She hoped she never lost that trait as she grew up.

"You ready to go, baby girl?" Annie asked.

"Yeah! Grammy and PopPop time!" Melanie yelled, then clomped her way as fast as she could go, which wasn't very fast, toward the garage.

Frankie chuckled and took the bag of snacks from her, kissing her temple. "I love you."

"I love you too," Annie said.

"Best thing that ever happened to me," Frankie muttered, more to himself than to Annie, and hurried to catch up to Melanie so he could help her into the car and into her safety seat in the back.

Annie took her time making sure all the lights were off before slowly heading for the garage herself. The house was a mess, she hadn't put the dishes away, and she was fairly sure there was still a load of clothes in the dryer. But that stuff didn't matter. Love did. Being with family. Making sure her husband knew how much she appreciated him. Making their daughter laugh. Telling her mom and dad how thankful she was for everything they'd done for her.

Life was good. Really good. And it had all started with meeting a little boy named Frankie when she was seven years old.

She could hear Melanie laughing out in the garage, and it made Annie smile. Her daughter might not have been the child she'd expected, but she was absolutely perfect in every way.

With a huge smile on her face, Annie went to join her husband and daughter.

Thank you ALL so much for loving Annie as much as I do. When I wrote Rescuing Emily I had no idea that Annie would be as appealing as she has...or as much fun to write and watch grow up!

You met a few characters in this book that come from my Delta Team Two series, so be sure to pick up *Shielding Gillian* if you haven't already (and yes, a younger Annie makes appearances in that series too!)

If you haven't already joined my *reader group (Susan Stoker's Stalkers) on Facebook, please do!*

JOIN my Newsletter and find out about sales, free books, contests and new releases before anyone else!!
http://www.stokeraces.com/contact-1.html

Deserving Cora (TBA)
Deserving Lara (TBA)
Deserving Maisy (TBA)
Deserving Ryleigh (TBA)

Delta Team Two Series

Shielding Gillian
Shielding Kinley
Shielding Aspen
Shielding Jayme (novella)
Shielding Riley
Shielding Devyn
Shielding Ember
Shielding Sierra

SEAL of Protection Series

Protecting Caroline
Protecting Alabama
Protecting Fiona
Marrying Caroline (novella)
Protecting Summer
Protecting Cheyenne
Protecting Jessyka
Protecting Julie (novella)
Protecting Melody
Protecting the Future
Protecting Kiera (novella)
Protecting Alabama's Kids (novella)
Protecting Dakota

SEAL of Protection: Legacy Series

Securing Caite
Securing Brenae (novella)
Securing Sidney
Securing Piper
Securing Zoey
Securing Avery
Securing Kalee
Securing Jane

SEAL Team Hawaii Series

Finding Elodie
Finding Lexie
Finding Kenna
Finding Monica (May 2022)
Finding Carly (Oct 2022)
Finding Ashlyn (May 2023)
Finding Jodelle (TBA)

Badge of Honor: Texas Heroes Series

Justice for Mackenzie
Justice for Mickie
Justice for Corrie
Justice for Laine (novella)
Shelter for Elizabeth
Justice for Boone
Shelter for Adeline
Shelter for Sophie
Justice for Erin
Justice for Milena
Shelter for Blythe
Justice for Hope

Shelter for Quinn
Shelter for Koren
Shelter for Penelope

Ace Security Series

Claiming Grace
Claiming Alexis
Claiming Bailey
Claiming Felicity
Claiming Sarah

Mountain Mercenaries Series

Defending Allye
Defending Chloe
Defending Morgan
Defending Harlow
Defending Everly
Defending Zara
Defending Raven

Silverstone Series

Trusting Skylar
Trusting Taylor
Trusting Molly
Trusting Cassidy

Stand Alone

Falling for the Delta
The Guardian Mist
Nature's Rift
A Princess for Cale

A Moment in Time- A Collection of Short Stories
Another Moment in Time- A Collection of Short Stories
Lambert's Lady

Special Operations Fan Fiction

http://www.AcesPress.com

Beyond Reality Series

Outback Hearts
Flaming Hearts
Frozen Hearts

Writing as Annie George:

Stepbrother Virgin (erotic novella)

ABOUT THE AUTHOR

New York Times, USA Today and *Wall Street Journal* Bestselling Author Susan Stoker has a heart as big as the state of Tennessee where she lives, but this all American girl has also spent the last fourteen years living in Missouri, California, Colorado, Indiana, and Texas. She's married to a retired Army man who now gets to follow *her* around the country.

She debuted her first series in 2014 and quickly followed that up with the SEAL of Protection Series, which solidified her love of writing and creating stories readers can get lost in.

If you enjoyed this book, or any book, please consider leaving a review. It's appreciated by authors more than you'll know.

www.stokeraces.com
www.AcesPress.com
susan@stokeraces.com